The House on the Hill

The House on the Hill

Eileen Dunlop

HOLIDAY HOUSE/NEW YORK

© Eileen Dunlop 1987
First published by Oxford University Press in 1987
Printed in the United States of America

Library of Congress Cataloging-in-Publication Data

Dunlop, Eileen.
The house on the hill.

SUMMARY: Cousins visiting proud, unfriendly Great-
aunt Jane in her spooky Victorian house come upon a
fifty-year-old mystery which is frightening in its
investigation and which reveals a tragic story in Jane's
past.
[1. Mystery and detective stories.   2. Supernatural—
Fiction.   3. Cousins—Fiction.   4. Great-aunts—Fiction]
I. Title.
PZ7.D9214Hr   1987   [Fic]   87-388
ISBN 0-8234-0658-X

For May Dunlop, aunt and friend

Contents

The House on the Hill

GILMORES

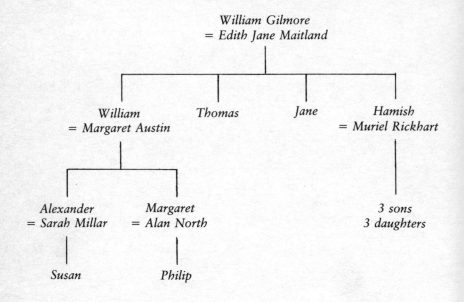

1

The House on the Hill

It was a fanciful name for a street in suburban Glasgow, Wisteria Avenue. For a start, it was not really an avenue at all, but a terrace, perched high on a hill overlooking the city, with large red sandstone houses planted along one side of it. They had fanciful names, too; *Winterwood, Linden Lea, St Aidan's, The Mount.* On the other side of the road there was a low wall, beyond which a grimy cliff, dotted with coarse grass and burdock, fell steeply into a gorge with a railway track at its foot. Here dusty trains shuttled to and fro, at no great speed, between Helensburgh and Glasgow Queen Street Station.

There was no Wisteria, either, nor had there been for as long as most of the people who lived there could remember. Not that that had been, for the majority, so very long. The vast Victorian mansions, built more than a century ago to house the families of wealthy shipbuilders and manufacturers, had more recently been converted into flats. The new owners had new ideas; they painted their flats in a modern way, and had uprooted the old gardens to make way for swimming pools, and patio areas, and barbecues, and garages for their cars. This was a pity, really, because their children would have loved the great, jungly gardens where other children had played, sixty, eighty, a hundred years ago.

There was only one jungle left now in the Avenue. It surrounded number twelve—*The Mount*—where Miss Jane Gilmore lived, and it grew wilder with every summer that passed. If there had ever been any Wisteria in that garden, it had long since been squeezed out by rusty aucubas and rhododendrons, and huge, raggy clumps of

1

pampas grass and bamboo. Even the old roses had grown so tall that their branches, laden with delicate pink and yellow blooms, scrambled to freedom over the boundary wall, dropping their pale petals on the pavement, and on the roof of the bus-shelter at the corner of Knightshill Road.

There was a time when Miss Gilmore used to come out occasionally, armed with shears and secateurs, and try to cut some of the jungle down, but in the last few years she seemed to have abandoned the struggle. The vegetation was now so high and dense that, from the road, you could not see any of the downstairs windows of the house at all. The rest of it, with pointed, church-like windows painted an ugly green, reared scowling out of the undergrowth, like a castle which might be enchanted, but not in any pleasantly romantic way.

More than once, it had been suggested to Miss Gilmore that she might make some money by having *The Mount* converted into flats. The Bowens at number six, she was assured, had made a small fortune. But resolutely she refused even to consider the idea. She was tired, and getting old, and was quite unable to face such an upheaval in her quiet life. What she did not know was that an upheaval of a different kind was just about to take place.

2

An Unwilling Guest

'I don't care what you say. You could have let me stay with the Cawleys.' His mother had not said anything, and Philip didn't expect her to, but he was determined to be provoking right to the bitter end. 'It's rotten of you, making me stay with your stuck-up old Aunt Jane. You've said yourself she hasn't a clue how to look after children.'

It was a calm afternoon at the end of September, when red maple leaves were drifting thinly in the gutters, sycamores hesitated between yellow and green, and the rosy sandstone mansions of Knightshill basked in the gentle warmth of the westering sun. It was a perfectly beautiful day, but as Philip North pushed his bicycle, with its precarious load of suitcase and school bag, up Cliff Road, he was not interested in the weather. He had been furious for three weeks, and he was furious now.

For as long as he could remember, Philip had heard no good of his great aunt, Jane Gilmore. He had heard her called proud, snobbish and unfriendly, vague, forgetful and unreliable, and incapable of looking after children— this last opinion having been voiced loudly by Philip's mother when she heard that her brother was sending his eleven-year-old daughter home from Kenya to go to school in Glasgow, and stay at *The Mount* with Aunt Jane. Recently Mrs North might have come to regret her frankness on this subject, but she could not deny the remarks she had made. Miss Gilmore's most recent sin was her failure to come to the funeral of Philip's father, earlier in the year; after that, Mrs North had said she would never speak to Aunt Jane again.

And yet now, only eight months later, here she was,

actually preparing to leave Philip with Aunt Jane, while she went off to London to do a term's course in Nursing. He had heard over and over again what a wonderful thing it was for her to have a place on the course, with a secure job in Glasgow at the end of it. Which was no doubt true, and Philip did not care terribly whether she went to London or not; what he objected to was being made to stay with old Aunt Jane, and Susan Gilmore, his cousin from Kenya. But when he bitterly reminded his mother of all the things she had said, and made her cry by pointing out that his father had refused to enter *The Mount,* she had no better reply than that they had no other family, and that she did not care to leave him with strangers. He could upset her, but he could not move her; she was tougher than she looked.

She was walking alongside him now, a thin little person with dark brown eyes and pale brown hair. The suitcase she was carrying was too heavy for her, and she had a strained, weary look which had come upon her in the summer before her husband died, and had never left her. Philip should have felt sorry for her, but he was too busy feeling sorry for himself. They turned out of Cliff Road, and walked the length of Wisteria Avenue with a blind of misunderstanding firmly drawn between them.

The Mount, or number twelve, was on the corner of the Avenue and the leafy, but busy Knightshill Road. Its front gate was signposted by a nasty black monkey-puzzle, of which Mrs North's grandfather had been extremely proud. Beyond it, the tangle of shrubs and small trees walled and overhung the path, making a deep tunnel between the gate and the front door. The gate stuck, but Philip kicked it open with unnecessary vigour, and ran his bicycle in over paving stones thinly furred with moss. While he took down his bags, his mother rang the bell; there was a long pause, then, just as Mrs North was about to ring again, the door opened, and Miss Jane Gilmore appeared, holding a china plate in one hand.

'Oh, it's you, Margaret,' she said, in the kind of voice which Philip despised as posh, although that really only meant that hers did not have as strong a Glasgow inflexion

4

as his own. 'I thought it might be the fish man.'

She was at first sight an unremarkable figure, a woman on the threshold of old age, in a blue dress. She was thin rather than fat, tall rather than small, frail rather than robust, but nothing unduly so. Her hair was an unruly mixture of black and grey, her face pale and tired, but not wrinkled, apart from lines on her broad forehead and around her mouth, which might have been engraved there with the finest of pointed tools. She had beautiful, unfaded brown eyes, set quite deeply in sockets which looked as if they had been defined very delicately with a sooty finger. Philip scarcely looked at her; at twelve and a half, he was blind to the beauty of the same eyes in his mother's face, and he felt no curiosity about his great Aunt Jane at all. He had seen her before, occasionally, when he and his mother had met her at the shops, and had then resented, vaguely, the patient way in which she had stopped to speak to them, as if she felt she must, but really would rather not.

Now she did not smile, and say, 'How nice to see you,' or even, 'Do come in,' but stood aside to let them enter, closing the door while they laid down Philip's luggage on the old red carpet. Philip had time to notice darkly varnished doors, and a wide stair rising up into shadow at the end of the hall, before a door was opened on the left, and he followed his mother into Miss Gilmore's sitting-room. It was a large room, with a bay window, but it seemed small because of all the enormous pieces of furniture crammed into it. Although the window was wide, the interior seemed gloomy, with brown velvet curtains inside, and outside un-pruned branches fingering the glass.

Philip sat down on a hard green sofa with silk tassels on its roly-poly arms. His mother, looking flustered, sat on the edge of a matching arm chair. Miss Gilmore sat, as if it were not worth settling, on the arm of another chair, and regarded them with grave, dark eyes. Without seeming rude, she made no attempt to start a conversation; perhaps she had lived so long in silence that it had ceased to bother her. It bothered Mrs North, who began to fill it, far too energetically.

'This is very good of you, Aunt Jane. I'm very grateful, I am really. Of course I'd have loved to take Philip to London with me, but I have to live in at the hospital. And although Mrs Balloch next door would have taken him if I'd asked her, well, I said to myself, if I have to go to London and leave Philip, I'd rather leave him with Aunt Jane, because at the end of the day, blood's thicker than water, isn't it? And he won't give you any trouble, Aunt Jane, will you, Philip?'

Without looking at Philip, who was in no mood to make promises, Miss Gilmore replied, 'He won't give me any trouble.' She did not say it hopefully, or threateningly; it was just a statement.

There was a longish pause, during which Philip watched his own foot trying to rub the pattern off the carpet. Then suddenly and unwisely, Mrs North asked, 'And where is Susan?' Philip winced as she looked around brightly, as if she expected Susan to emerge from behind one of the sofas.

'In the train, I suppose,' said Miss Gilmore flatly. 'If this is Tuesday, she has a Music lesson after school. If it's Wednesday, she goes to hockey. Either way, she's late back.'

'It's Tuesday,' said Mrs North. 'I, um—I hoped I might see her. But I'll just have to wait until December, when I come back to fetch Philip, won't I?'

Miss Gilmore did not answer this question, but the answer she might have given seemed to hover between them on the air.

'She has been living here for more than two years. You live less than a mile away. You might have seen her any time you liked.'

Philip carefully traced a curly shape on the carpet with his toe.

Fortunately, at that moment, the doorbell rang again. Miss Gilmore said, 'That will be the fish now,' and went out into the hall. Mrs North rose in some confusion, gathering up her bag and scarf.

'I'll have to go, love,' she said to Philip.

6

Philip had really intended to persevere in his huffiness, to punish his mother finally by letting her go without making friends, but inconveniently, at the last moment, he did feel sorry for her. Since his father had died at the end of January, she had hardly ever bothered to make up her face, or go to the hairdresser. With the best of intentions, she always got everything wrong. He looked at her now, and saw her tired, and unhappy, and small. As she fumbled in her bag, looking for a ten pound note to give him, Philip strode over to her, and gave her a rough, silent hug. On the verge of tears, she broke away from him, and he could hear her voice in the hall, high and unnatural, as she said goodbye to her aunt. Philip swore under his breath.

When Miss Gilmore came back, which was not immediately, she said without looking at him, 'If you'd like to come upstairs, I'll show you your room.' Polite, but distant. A bit like in a hotel, Philip thought. Only less anxious to please.

The Mount was a house on three floors, if you counted the attics. Carrying his suitcases—she had picked up his school bag—Philip staggered after Miss Gilmore up the wide, red carpeted staircase, into darkness punctured only by the eerie light which filtered through a stained glass window on the half landing. Their footfalls made little impression on the great, hanging silence of the house, and Philip, who was used to small, light places, shivered a little. He would not, he thought, enjoy going up to bed here alone. They emerged at the top of the stairs onto a wide, dim landing, with closed doors on two sides, and, in the wall opposite, two shadowy entrances to passages from which other rooms must open. Philip hoped that his room was not along a spooky, unlit passage, but, just as he was forming the thought, he realised that it was not. Miss Gilmore had opened a door at the end of the balustrade which ran along the edge of the stair well, revealing a narrow flight of steps, rising between whitewashed walls. There was no carpet here, only old green linoleum, and he knew, with a spurt of annoyance, that he was destined for one of the attic rooms at the top of the house.

Philip had lived all his life in a modern, semi-detached house, but he had heard enough about this place, where his mother had been brought up, to know that he was going to sleep in a servant's bedroom. There had been no servants living in the house while his mother was growing up, but, away back in his grandfather's childhood, maids had slept in little, sparsely furnished rooms, poked in under the roof. Philip's father had said it was a damned disgrace, the way people like the Gilmores had exploited the poor. As he shuffled upwards with his suitcases, pique wiped out, for the moment, the feelings of unease and loneliness which he had experienced on the stairs below.

The attic stair came out upon a small, bare landing, with four little brown doors. Miss Gilmore opened one of them.

'We have supper at half-past six,' she said, putting down Philip's bag on the wooden floor. 'But come down when you like.'

Then she went off downstairs again, her feet clopping over the linoleum, muffled as they reached the carpet on the main landing.

Angrier than ever, Philip unpacked in the tiny, coomed bedroom, so tiny that there was only room for a narrow bed, a chest of drawers and a wooden chair. Of course, he told himself, she meant to insult him, that snooty old Aunt Jane, trying to get her own back because his mother didn't visit her, or invite her to their house for tea. Which served her right for being so uppity, and not wanting his mother to marry his father. Philip had been brought up on the story of how Margaret Gilmore's family had wanted her to marry someone rich and grand, from a family like their own, and how she had defied them to marry the poor man she loved, Alan North, a bank clerk whose father had laboured in the shipyards of the Clyde. So it was easy to believe now that Miss Jane Gilmore, the last of that snobbish, wealthy clan, was trying to take her revenge by scorning the bank clerk's son.

What was more difficult to believe was that he was actually here at all, considering all the hard things he had heard said in the past, and when both Mrs Balloch and

8

Mrs Cawley would gladly have looked after him. Philip could not know how his mother, lonely now that her husband was dead, yearned for some family relationship on which she could rely, and how she had hoped, in her muddling way, that Philip might somehow be the means of bringing her and her aunt closer together. Or that now she was walking home alone through the Park, with tears in her eyes, thinking how very foolish that hope had been.

When he had finished stowing away his clothes, Philip sat on the bed, reading a comic, and failing to notice the comfortable mattress and nice green duvet. He kept an eye on his watch and at half-past six went downstairs, whistling and clattering in defiance of the dark. There was a light on in the room opposite the sitting-room, so he went in.

3
Supper Time

This was the dining-room, and it was another awful place. There was more, enormous, dark furniture. A sideboard with cupboards that Philip could have got inside. A table, laid for three, which could have seated fourteen without crowding. A glass-fronted bookcase with carved fruit on top, and round baby faces peeping out of leaves. A vast black marble chimney piece supporting bronze horses, with a great, gilt-framed looking glass above it, so high that you would have needed a ladder to see yourself. And underneath it, an incongruously modern gas fire. There were heavily framed pictures, hung closely together on the dark red walls, Highland cows uttering frozen moos by Highland waterholes, hounds slavering at the throat of a wall-eyed stag.

'God's truth,' said Philip, under his breath, and, as he said it, caught the eye of a very disapproving personage in a portrait, who obviously took a poor view of swearing. 'And I bet these ruddy pictures were his, too,' Philip thought—but avoided catching his eye again.

There were signs, however, that this room was lived in as the sitting-room across the hall was not. Philip noticed well-worn but comfortable arm chairs, one on either side of a striped hearthrug, and on a small table beside one of them, a modern Anglepoise lamp, books, spectacles and letters. There were a few magazines, and today's newspaper on the floor. As he was warming his behind at the fire, and trying idly to read the headlines upside down, Miss Gilmore came into the room through a door to the left of the fireplace. She was carrying a casserole, on a tray.

10

'Sit here, please,' she said to Philip, as she put it down on the table, and then called over her shoulder, 'Susan! Supper's ready!'

Somewhere, far away, Philip heard a door bang, then a light running of feet, and Susan Gilmore, the rich cousin from Kenya, came skidding into the room. She looked guardedly at Philip, and said, 'Hi.'

'Hi,' responded Philip, unenthusiastically.

Miss Gilmore did not seem to think it necessary to introduce them. While Susan was sliding onto a chair opposite Philip's, and unrolling her napkin, she casually ladled platefuls of stew, and pushed them down the table. The children ate for a while in silence, watching each other; Miss Gilmore moved a tiny quantity of food around her plate with a fork, and presently abandoned it. She did not look at Philip, and, for the moment, he did not look at her.

Philip had come determined to dislike Susan, so it was not difficult for him to decide quickly that she was plain. She had short black hair and dark, Gilmore eyes in a thin face which, as she stared back at Philip, was expressionless. She was wearing a brown skirt and cream blouse, with a striped school tie; Philip, whose father had not approved of schools with uniforms, eyed her clothes with disfavour. But, as she did not speak to him, and he had no intention of speaking to her, he lost interest, turning his attention—he could hardly help it—to the fierce gentleman above the sideboard, the one who had seemed so outraged by Philip's whispered oath.

He really was a disturbing old fellow, immobilised though he was in his dull gold frame. Up to his shoulders, he was encased stiffly in a heavy black suit; above the suit his red face sprang confidently out of a high white collar. His hands, importantly fingering an ornate gold chain which hung around his neck, had been caught in mid-fidget by an artist good at painting hands. His grey whiskers stood up stiffly, and he had the kind of painted eyes which seem to be watching you every time you glance up. More than once, Philip tried to be brave, and stare him

11

out, but each time he was obliged to drop his eyelids to avoid the old man's aggressive glare.

When the first course was finished, the plates were removed to the sideboard by Susan, who brought to the table a succulent apple crumble. Again Miss Gilmore helped the two children, liberally but absent-mindedly, and ate nothing herself. It was a great surprise to Philip to discover that she was such a good cook, and something of a relief as well. While the pudding was being eaten, she and Susan did not exactly have a conversation, but some remarks were dropped into a silence which neither of them seemed to mind.

'I saw the blackbirds today. Do you suppose they'll nest in the coal cellar again next year?'

'You didn't throw out their old welly, did you?'

'I never throw anything out. I'm famous for it.'

'I'd forgotten. So you are.'

Later,

'Listen, Jane. You got five and a half out of fifteen for that Latin exercise you helped me with. I think I'll do it on my own next time.'

'Please yourself. Fifty years is a long time for forgetting Latin.'

And, at the end of the meal,

'Oh, honestly, Jane! Have you eaten *anything* today?'

'To be sure. I had lunch with Jo—her Hebridean fish pie. She stood over me until I swallowed it. It was awful.'

Once again, Philip was surprised. After hearing so much about Miss Gilmore's inability to cope with children, he had not expected to find her and Susan companionable. Nor could he fail to notice the anxiety in Susan's voice, or the distress on her sallow little face, as she removed Miss Gilmore's untouched supper from the table. Though why she should care, he did not know.

When Philip had finished his third helping of apple crumble, Susan said she was going to do her homework, and departed upstairs. Philip hung around with his hands in his pockets until Miss Gilmore had cleared the

12

sideboard, then he pointed to the portrait, and said abruptly, 'Who's that old geezer?'

'My father,' she replied.

'Oh.' Momentarily, Philip was abashed, but then he remembered that it didn't matter whether her feelings were hurt, after the mean way she had treated him. So he went on, 'Anyway, I was wondering. Do you think I could sit where I can't see him? I don't like the look of him, and I keep catching his eye.'

Miss Gilmore nodded thoughtfully.

'That's what Susan said,' she told him. 'When she first came, she used to sit where you've been sitting, and he made her so nervous that it put her off her food. Or so she said. Sit where you like. There's plenty of room.'

'Does he make you nervous?' Philip couldn't resist asking.

'No,' she said. 'He stopped making me nervous when he died.'

4

Burglars and Bedrooms

For fear of having to help her wash up, Philip did not follow Miss Gilmore out to the kitchen. Feeling that he could hardly walk uninvited into the sitting-room, on the first night, and switch on the television, he decided that he might as well go upstairs and get ready for bed. It was now dark outside, and the thought of the vast empty house above and around him, with so many lonely stairs to climb, made him very uneasy. Better to go up now, and get it over. He had seen a bathroom door open on the landing as he came down, so he decided that he would go to the loo now, and hope that he would not have to go again before morning. He would not bother about washing tonight; his mother was not there to chivvy him, and Philip felt that you could overdo that kind of thing. So, tunelessly whistling, he began to climb the stair.

The darkness reached down to enfold him. When the stair turned back on itself at the half landing, he could not even see the steps, so it was all the more noticeable, the thin ribbon of light shining under a door on his left, just as he reached the main landing. Susan's room, he reflected bitterly. Wealthy Aunt Jane's wealthy little favourite. She would be sitting in there now, in her fancy school uniform, doing her Latin exercises by the fire. She would have a nice lamp, and a radio, and an electric blanket, and a window with a view, instead of a grubby skylight with a chimney stack outside. It wasn't fair.

He found the loo; it was an incredibly old-fashioned one, with blue enamelled flowers in the bowl, and a chain hanging from a high cistern. When he pulled the chain, the gurgling and swooshing were so awful that Philip began to

14

giggle with sheer nerves; he fled up the dark attic stairs, dashed into his room, and closed the door. When he had recovered, he got undressed, climbed into bed, and opened this week's *Beano,* which he had not yet read.

The gurgling in the water pipes ceased, and night gathered itself within the house in a silence which was the more intimate because beyond it was sound, the muted roar of traffic which was ever in the background of city life. Philip got warm. He had had a long, exhausting day, and he was beginning to feel sleepy, when suddenly something terrible happened. Behind the head of his bed, he heard a noise. Two noises, indeed, unmistakable. The click of a light switch. The opening of a cupboard door. There was someone in the room next to his.

Philip's only thought was that this must be a burglar. There were more burglaries in this part of Glasgow than anywhere else in Scotland. You had to pay extra insurance. A burglar had got in while they were having supper, and had made his way to the top of the house, intending to work downwards. Dry-mouthed but clear-headed, Philip considered alternatives. There was no point in calling for help—the only other occupants of the house, far away below, were an old woman and a little girl. There was no point in bolting—he would be heard and caught and knifed before he got to the foot of the attic stair. But he certainly could not lie quaking in bed either, because, when the burglar had finished where he was, *he would come in here.* As this unpleasant fact sank in, he heard sounds again. A creak, as a door closed, then feet padding across the floor.

Then Philip did something very brave, although afterwards he said he had only done it because it seemed better than waiting to be murdered in his bed. On his chest of drawers, there was an old-fashioned brass candlestick, long and heavy. He slipped out of bed, lifted it down, and without giving himself time to think any more, cautiously opened his door. He tiptoed over the cold floorboards to the next door, and violently threw it open.

'Hands up!' he yelled absurdly, charging forward, and

found himself standing on a green carpet, blinking in the light of a pink-shaded lamp. He had a confused impression of white walls, with bookshelves and posters, and striped curtains, then Susan's voice said in astonishment, 'Philip, for heaven's sake! What on earth do you think you're doing?'

Philip stood staring at her, with the candlestick in his hand. The relief and the surprise and the sense of foolishness were overwhelming, his knees shook, and, to his horror, he thought he was going to burst into tears. He took an enormous, gulping breath, and tried to explain. 'I heard noises. I thought—I thought it was a burglar.'

Susan, who was sitting at a desk in her pink dressing-gown, got up and came over to him. She took the candlestick out of his hand, and pushed him down gently onto a brown corduroy bean bag, on one side of a small fireplace. 'You have had a fright, haven't you?' she said, peering sideways into his white face as she bent down to switch on the electric fire. 'But did you really think it was a burglar? How fantastically brave of you to come flying in with the candlestick. I'd never have dared.'

The warm admiration in her voice was balm to him. He had never been so scared in his life. Now he began to feel better, and managed to say, 'I thought I was on my own up here. When I came upstairs, I saw a light under a door, at the top of the first flight. I though it was your room—only, of course, it couldn't have been,' he concluded lamely, but with a puzzled expression in his blue eyes.

Philip was aware of a sudden quickening of attention in Susan as he said this, and he looked straight at her, for the first time since his dramatic arrival in her room. She had dropped down onto a cushion, on the other side of the fire, and was sitting hugging her knees, with a speculative expression on her thin brown face.

'No, it couldn't have been,' she agreed. 'I suppose Jane forgot to tell you I was up here too—she doesn't have the best memory in the world, poor lamb. Or maybe she just thought that since I was the one who insisted on having you here, it was up to me to tell you the arrangement. But

16

never mind that, for the moment. Listen, Philip, are you sure you saw a light under that door? Are you sure, positive?'

Philip bridled, just a little. He had just got over feeling foolish, and he didn't like the notion that now she was doubting his word.

'Yes,' he said, emphatically. 'Sure, positive. It was very clear, in the darkness. Someone must have left the light on. Aunt Jane, if her memory's so terrible.'

Susan shook her dark head.

'No, it wasn't that,' she said.

'Well, then, it must have been a street light outside, shining in through the window. That might show, because the landing's so dark. Well, mightn't it?' demanded Philip challengingly, seeing from her face that she didn't think a lot of this explanation either.

Susan stretched out her bare feet along the carpet, and said, 'There isn't any street light. But it's all right. Keep your cool. I'm not doubting your word. This is all very interesting to me, because I've seen that light too.'

'Well, then,' Philip began again, but this time Susan interrupted him.

'No, hold on, Philip, please. The point is that it's impossible. You see, that room is completely empty. When Jane's father died, she was left with this enormous house, and very little money. It's why she can't afford to get the garden attended to, or the outside of the place repainted. And every so often, she has to sell something to pay the rates, which are horrific. Apparently that room was her father's drawing-room, and had some valuable furniture and paintings in it. Well, just after I came here to stay, she sold the lot, and men came from Phillips', and took it all away in a van. Since then, the room has been empty, and all the electric light bulbs have been taken out. And there's no street light, I do assure you. Queer, isn't it?'

'Not half,' agreed Philip. He would have suspected anyone else of pulling his leg, but Susan was obviously sincere. And, after all, he had seen the light with his own eyes. 'Has Aunt Jane seen it?' he asked presently.

17

Susan lifted her thin shoulders slightly.

'I don't know,' she admitted. 'I think probably not. She sleeps on the ground floor, and she has a bathroom off her bedroom, so I don't think she often has any reason to come upstairs at night. And the light isn't always there. I've certainly never spoken to her about it—Jane isn't someone I'd care to worry without very good reason.'

But Philip was not interested in talking about Miss Gilmore. There was a more pressing question on his mind.

'Susan,' he said, 'do you think this house is haunted?'

He watched her considering this very seriously.

'I'm not sure,' she said eventually. 'I've never actually seen a ghost, although that doesn't mean there aren't any. And although I get spooky feelings on the stair, that's just imagination, or suggestion, isn't it? But—well, it has been a very unhappy house, and I think you can feel it. So many sad people have lived here—it's as if the house remembers. It's haunted by memories, I suppose. But the light under the door is another matter. I don't understand that at all.'

Philip found this far from reassuring, and he wondered how Susan endured being up here on her own, night after night, if this was how she really felt.

'Why does Aunt Jane make you sleep up here,' he enquired, 'when there are so many bedrooms downstairs?'

It appeared that he had been mistaken in supposing that Miss Gilmore wanted to insult him personally, but what if she were trying to insult them both?

But, 'Oh, she doesn't make me,' Susan assured him. 'Jane never makes anyone do anything they don't want to do. When I came, she said I could sleep anywhere I liked, and she showed me lots of bedrooms—awful, stuffy places, with velvet curtains and beds like those things in churches they put coffins on. What d'you call them? Catafalques. I'd have gone mad. So I said I'd sleep up here, because it seemed to me this was the only place in the house where happy people had lived.'

'Happy people?' echoed Philip, at a loss to understand.

'Yes. When Jane was a little girl, a housemaid called Maggie Brown used to sleep in this room. She was always getting into trouble for laughing and singing, and she even gave cheek to Jane's father, which must have made her unique. But she did it once too often, and got the sack. Then Jo came. I don't know what her surname was then, but she's Mrs Jo Wilcox now. She stopped living here years ago, when she married the gardener from next door, but she still comes three mornings a week—more often if Jane needs her. She's such a kindly, loyal soul—I don't know what on earth Jane would do without her. I think she's the only person left in the world Jane really loves.' A somewhat wistful expression crossed Susan's face, but then she went on, 'You'll find I'm right, Philip. It isn't a bit scary up here. Once you're up. That's why I thought you'd prefer it to a posh room downstairs. The only other place in this house that feels nice is Jane's bedroom, but that's just Jane.'

Philip had no idea how to reply to this, so he changed the subject, saying, 'Your room's a lot nicer than mine.' It came out sounding more accusing than he had meant it to.

'Have a heart,' said Susan, half indignantly. 'I live here all the time. But it is nice, isn't it? I painted it myself, and Jo made the curtains for me, and helped me to put up the shelves. Jane gave me the carpet, and I bought the rest of the stuff myself—my Dad gives me a good allowance. It's easier than being a good father, I suppose.'

'Isn't he a good father?'

Susan pondered for a moment, then she said, 'He's fun to be with, occasionally. A good entertainer, you know, if he hasn't got anything better to do. But he hates the idea of being responsible for anyone else. I sometimes feel years older than him. What about yours? Or would you rather not talk about it?'

Then Philip, who was warm and relaxed, was tempted to let it all come tumbling out, about the rows and the shouting, and the impossibility of ever pleasing a man who wanted you to be exactly like him in every way, and never gave you room to breathe or grow the way you wanted to. And how he had shouted back, and defied him, and how, now that he was dead, the pain and the guilt were

19

sometimes almost too much to bear. But he still couldn't talk about it to anybody, and shook his copper-coloured head.

'Well, never mind,' said Susan kindly.

They sat quietly for a while, warming their toes by the fire. Nearby, a church clock struck nine.

'That's St Kentigern's,' said Susan. 'The church Jane fails to attend. Listen, Philip. I'll have to finish my homework now, or there'll be hell to pay tomorrow. But before you go—what are we going to do about that queer room downstairs?'

Philip was pleased, afterwards, that he had risen immediately to the challenge.

'Investigate,' he replied firmly. 'Tomorrow, after school.'

'Great,' said Susan, well satisfied. 'There's no hockey, so I'll be home early.' She had seated herself at her desk again, and was unscrewing the cap of her fountain pen. Philip was outside the door when, suddenly, she called him back. 'Hi, Philip.'

'What is it?'

'Don't tell me if you don't want to—but why does your mother never come to see Jane?'

Philip saw no reason not to tell her this.

'It's not her. It was my Dad. He didn't like the Gilmores, because he thought they didn't want my Mum to marry him.'

'Ah. Pity,' Susan said.

5

The Empty Room

When Philip came back from school next day, he found some changes in his room. There was a small, rather rickety bamboo table beside the bed, with a reading lamp on top of his great pile of comics. On the floor lay a blue fluffy rug, and, covering a large area of the faded pink wallpaper there was a poster, showing two gorillas in close-up, and underneath the words, 'Love Me'. Susan, thought Philip, as he looked around. He knew that she was home, because he had seen her school coat and beret hanging in the vestibule as he came in.

It was ungrateful of him not to feel pleased, but, now that he had had time to think, he was rather regretting the friendly session he had had with Susan the previous evening. He felt that he would have been better to have kept to his original plan of keeping his distance. He had to admit that she had been nice when he had made a fool of himself over the burglar business, hadn't laughed, and had told him warmly how brave he was; on the other hand, it was her fault, and silly old Aunt Jane's, that he'd had such a fright at all. They should have told him at supper what the sleeping arrangements were, instead of wittering on in their posh voices about blackbirds and Latin marks. Philip scarcely knew what Latin was, but his father had said it was a waste of time. Besides, Susan was a Gilmore, the daughter of a man who hadn't wanted his sister to marry Philip's father. He was thankful that he hadn't confided in Susan about life at home, but, very unfairly, was ready to blame her for trying to worm confidences out of him. And he was not going to be grateful for a few shabby bits of junk, so she needn't expect to be thanked. He had got this

21

far with his unpleasant train of thought when the door opened, and Susan put her black head round it.

'Hi, Sunshine,' she greeted him. 'How d'you like your home comforts? I got them out of the box Jane keeps for Jumble Sales. But then when somebody comes to the door asking for jumble, she can never remember where she put the box. I could have got you something posher, but I don't like to rifle the tombs of the dead downstairs. Now, what about that spooky room, before the light fails?'

Philip looked at her in exasperation. If she went on like this, it was going to be uphill work disliking her.

Susan had changed into jeans and a jersey, which Philip was already wearing. She was carrying a cardboard folder and an exercise book with a pen attached, and had a small, old-fashioned camera with a flash gun slung around her neck.

'For collecting evidence, and starting a file on the case,' she explained.

'Won't Aunt Jane mind us poking around like this?' Philip asked, as they descended the attic stairs.

'Oh, no. She's not that kind of person,' said Susan. 'If she was, I'd have asked her first.'

The door at the head of the shadowy staircase was very tall and heavy, as Philip turned the smooth black knob, and pushed it open. As it swung gently back on its hinges, the children found themselves in an empty room which seemed to them as high and wide as a church. This impression was accentuated by the tapering upper sashes of the windows; the Wisteria Avenue houses had been built at a period when Gothic architecture was enjoying a revival. Susan and Philip were of normal size for their age, but in this space they felt very, very small. Far away from them, at the other end, the deep bay window was still draped with the snuffy-brown velvet curtains which had obviously appealed to someone, once upon a time; from the shabby, corniced ceiling a cobwebby grey chandelier drooped disconsolately, and above the white marble fireplace hung a huge, tarnished looking-glass, similar to the one in the dining-room. Apart from these items, the room was stripped bare. Only outlines were visible against the walls of pieces of furniture which had once stood there, around darker patches where the sun's rays had been unable to reach. The late afternoon sun slanted in now through the smutty windows, sending a dusty shaft of light across the floorboards.

'There's nothing here,' said Philip, his voice running thinly away from him down the room.

'Nonsense,' replied Susan crisply. 'Don't be such a defeatist. We haven't even started looking yet. Now, you take the fireplace side, and I'll start at the door. And mind you look properly. You never know.'

Which was all very well, but it is extremely difficult to ransack an empty room. Even more so, if you haven't a clue what you're looking for. Philip looked down the cracks between the floorboards. He ran his fingers along the space between the skirting board and the wall, and thrust his head into the dead, cold fireplace. Feeling inventive, he even pulled out the little iron drawer which had caught the ashes of fires at which Miss Gilmore's father had once warmed his slippered feet. It had been emptied and swept clean long ago. But, as he passed the hearth, in the corner between it and the window wall, he came to a door, which he had not particularly noticed before.

'What do you suppose this is?' he asked Susan. 'Cupboard?'

She came over from the window, where she was investigating, fruitlessly and with sneezes, the brown velvet curtains.

'Let's open it and see,' she said.

But it was not a cupboard. The door opened inwards, and Philip and Susan found themselves staring into a bedroom, stuffy, overdraped, with huge, glass-fronted wardrobes, and the kind of bed which Susan had described as a catafalque. It had a dark, carved headboard, and a purple satin quilt, and it dominated the room quite horribly. There was, not exactly a smell, but a sourness in the atmosphere, suggesting illness and decay; the contrast with the spacious, naked room next door was stunning. The children stood in silence on the dark carpet, while a large blue fly buzzed drunkenly between the purple curtains and the tightly sealed window panes.

'This must have been his bedroom,' whispered Philip, when he had got his wind again. 'Him in the portrait. Maybe he died in here,' he added ghoulishly.

'No. He died in a nursing home,' said Susan flatly. 'Jo told me. Finally the doctor insisted he should be carted away before Jane broke her back trying to lift him. He was—well, demented, latterly, and he wouldn't let anyone else near him. Oh, let's get out of here, Philip. What a horrible place!'

They went back into the empty room, closing the door quietly behind them. Subdued, and feeling that their search had been hopeless, they stood by the window, looking out at the garden which rampaged all along the side of the house, a tree-ringed wilderness of withering weeds and unpruned roses, with the fluffy remains of summer's rosebay willow herb spiking what had once been lawns and a tennis court. From the great bough of a chestnut tree, the rotting remains of a swing hung unevenly, and among the rosebeds was the basin of a dried-up pool. Its lilies were long dead, and it was half-filled now with greyish silt and decaying leaves. The shortening day was over; the sun had moved a little to the west since they first entered, and was now going down redly, filling the garden and the room behind them with dull, fiery light.

'It's the old rose garden,' said Susan. 'All the Gilmore children used to play in it. I suppose your Mum and my Dad were the last.'

But Philip was looking at something else.

'What's that place in the corner, beside the wall?' he asked, pointing to a small stone building, much overgrown with ivy and columbine.

'I don't know. A summer house, I suppose,' said Susan, with a trace of impatience in her voice. She stood biting her lip, with a small frown between her dark brows, then she burst out with passion, 'Oh, God, Philip, isn't it awful? If only poor old Jane could make up her mind to sell it all, while it's still in a fit state for anyone to buy, and get herself a little flat on the South Side, or a nice cottage down the Clyde. She'd be so much better off.'

'Then why doesn't she?' enquired Philip, not understanding.

Susan turned away from the window, and sat down on the stripped window seat, with her back to the ravaged garden. She shook her head, and sighed.

'She doesn't seem able to make up her mind to it,' she told him. 'She knows she'd be far better out of here, but she just can't get herself to the point of setting things in motion. She has no—initiative, I think it's called. It isn't her fault. She isn't well, and she's had such an awful life. I think it must have drained all her energy.'

This was news to Philip. He had heard nothing of Jane Gilmore except that she was vague in her manner but proud, couldn't cope with children, and hadn't wanted his mother to marry his father.

But what he asked was, 'Can't she smile?'

Susan observed him closely before she replied, as if she were trying to decide whether this might be a frivolous, or perhaps even a nasty question. But she must have concluded that it was neither, because she answered as if she thought he really cared.

'Isn't it dreadful?' she said. 'I honestly don't think she can. I asked my Dad about it once, and he said she didn't have any sense of humour, but that simply isn't true. Sometimes she tells me the most hilarious stories, and I can see her enjoying watching me laughing, but she never laughs herself. And if I tell her something funny that happened at school—she went to the same place herself, away back in the Thirties—I can often sense that she's amused, but she can't laugh with me. I think that probably she has been so unhappy for so long that she has—well, sort of crawled away inside herself, and hidden from people who laugh normally, and have fun.' Susan turned her head, and glanced out into the garden. 'It's odd you should mention this,' she told Philip, turning back to face him.

25

'Why?'

'Well, that swing out there reminded me, just a few minutes ago. The nearest I've ever seen Jane to smiling was one day about a fortnight ago. She'd been out somewhere in the afternoon, and I met her in Cliff Road when I was coming home from school. It was down where Cliff Road turns into Almondbank, and there's a big chestnut tree on the corner. Some quite little children were playing there. Some of them were up in the branches giggling in the leaves, and some of them were swinging on a rope they'd tied to a branch, and falling into a sand pit. They were helpless laughing, the way young kids sometimes are, and Jane was standing on the pavement watching them, with such a tender, amused expression on her face. Then two of the kids jumped down, and came running over to talk to her. And I thought she was going to smile, and answer them, but she didn't. She just turned, and walked away quite quickly, almost as if she was frightened. Then she was unwell in the evening. It's all very tragic, really, but I don't know what's to be done. She doesn't confide in me.'

Once again, Philip did not know how to reply. Susan had been mistaken in supposing him sympathetic; he was merely curious, and quite unpractised in caring as much for any other human being as he realised Susan cared for Jane. He had always thought that grown-ups were supposed to care for children, not the other way round. He stood squinting uncertainly into Susan's sombre face, but, before he could put an answer together, suddenly her mood changed. Jumping up from the window seat she said, 'Come on. Since we haven't found anything to photograph for the file, I'll take your picture. In the haunted room. Stand down there by the wall, and look haunted.'

Perhaps it was because of the sadness of the last half hour, perhaps because tension had been released by their failure to find any obvious mystery behind the dark door, but instantaneously they became silly. Susan took a photograph of Philip doing an ape impression against the wall. Philip took one of Susan walking on her hands with a notebook in her mouth. Susan took one of Philip with his head up the chimney. He took one of her wrapped in a skirt of velvet curtain, imitating an opera singer, with her mouth wide open. When the roll of film ran out, they went upstairs to get ready for supper.

'I'll take the film to the Rushasnap shop in Blantyre Road, on my way home from school tomorrow,' said Susan. 'With any luck, we'll get the prints on Friday. You can send one to your Mum. I expect she's missing you dreadfully.'

And now Philip did feel ashamed. For he had been so absorbed in his own affairs that he had not thought of his mother once, in the twenty-four hours since she left him.

6

Gilmores

Later that evening, when Susan and Philip were going upstairs together, the clear white line of light was once again visible under the door of the empty drawing room. They stopped on the landing, and stared at it in perplexity.

'It occurs to me,' remarked Susan, 'that there would be one quick way of putting an end to this mystery. We could open the door now, and go in.'

Philip made a soft, exploding sound with his lips in the darkness.

'No chance,' he said, definitely. 'I'd never dare. Never in a thousand years. Would you?'

'Er—no,' Susan said, and they went on upstairs to bed.

The next two days passed uneventfully. Philip and Susan went their separate ways to school in the autumn chill of morning, and returned in the amber sunlight of leafy afternoons. Away from Wisteria Avenue, Philip's life went on as usual, dominated by football, punctuated by tickings-off from his teacher, Mr Grainger, and enlivened by Miss Gilmore's packed lunches, which were the envy and wonder of the whole class. Back at *The Mount*, although he still panicked irrationally every time he had to climb the stairs alone, and although the profound, timeless silence of the house continued to oppress him, he slept well, and agreed with Susan that the attic rooms felt safe and benign. Which might, as she suggested, be because happy people had once lived in them.

As for the unhappy person downstairs—Philip supposed, after what Susan had told him, that she was unhappy, and certainly her gravity was unnatural—he saw very little of her. A breakfast of eggs, with bacon or sausages, was waiting for the children on the hot-plate when they rushed downstairs at half-past seven, but by that time Miss Gilmore had taken her morning tea back to bed. Her suppers, as well as her packed lunches, were delicious, and, to that extent, Philip felt that people were wrong in saying that she didn't know how to look after children. Feeding, he reckoned, was the most important part of looking after. What she obviously didn't know, or care to find out, was how children expected to be treated by the adults in their lives, with the mixture of bossiness and indulgence which made them feel secure. She did not put on any special voice or face for Susan's or Philip's benefit; on the odd occasion when she spoke to either of them, she did so as she would have spoken to someone of her own age. Susan obviously didn't mind this, but she had been living at *The Mount* for two years. Philip found that it took a bit of getting used to.

However, it was neither Miss Gilmore's mode of address nor her silence which really unnerved Philip, it was the fact that she hardly ever looked at him. When they met in the hall, or on the pavement outside, when they were together in the dining-room in the evening, even if she was giving him a plate, or asking him to pass the salt, her dark eyes avoided his, and he was all the time more certain that it was deliberate. It was very strange, and, in some way, upsetting; he had come here with the intention of being offhand, and ignoring her, but he had not expected her to take the lead by being offhand, and ignoring him. Adults were not supposed to treat children like that, and he objected to her breaking the rules. When they went up to their rooms on Thursday evening, Philip followed Susan into hers, and asked why she thought he was being treated as if he were not there: Susan said she hadn't really noticed, and was very surprised.

'But I'm sure she isn't doing it on purpose, Philip,' she said, and Philip thought crossly that he might have known she would come to the defence of her precious Jane. 'She's such a gentle creature, she'd never mean to hurt anybody. Maybe it just seems as if she isn't looking at you properly.

She's shy with strangers, and she has very poor eyesight. Unless—'

'Unless what?' demanded Philip, who thought the defence pretty feeble, so far.

Susan perched on the edge of her desk, and looked at him pensively.

'Unless,' she said slowly, 'you perhaps remind her of somebody—from long ago. You remember, the other evening, we were talking about ghosts. Well, it occurred to me afterwards that Jane is probably more at risk when it comes to seeing ghosts than we are. I'm supposed to look very much as Jane did, when she was my age, and sometimes I see her looking at me in a strange, recognising sort of way, as if perhaps she sees the ghost of her own young self in me.' Susan paused, then added seriously, 'Look, Philip. I realise that to you Jane may seem a batty old thing—I suspect she does to most people. But when you know her better, you'll realise that the marvel is that she's completely sane. I'll tell you what happened to her, one day.'

'I'm supposed to look like my Dad,' said Philip, preferring to pass over these last remarks.

Susan gave him a rather cool look. 'Oh, I see,' she said, as she began to take her homework books out of her bag. 'It can't be that, then, can it?'

But privately, Philip was not so sure. When he looked in a mirror, he could never see the slightest resemblance between his own square-jawed, blue-eyed, bronze-thatched head and his father's long, grey-eyed, thin-brown-haired one.

On Friday, Susan came home with the news that the photographs were not ready. The Rushasnap man was just back from Majorca, and had a backlog of orders. They would be ready tomorrow, in the early afternoon.

'I'll fetch them on my way back from hockey,' said Susan. 'We're playing Dollar Academy away, so I won't be back much before three.'

Supper that evening was even quieter than it had been before. Once again the food was excellent, but Miss Gilmore did not speak once, and Philip, now sitting beside

30

Susan with his back to the sideboard, kept glancing with rising annoyance at her pale, withdrawn face. Because, he told himself firmly, he had no intention of starting to feel sorry for Aunt Jane, whatever Susan might say about her unhappy life. Philip had troubles of his own, and had to put up with them; she could do the same. So he glared at her between mouthfuls.

But when the meal, of which Miss Gilmore had eaten next to nothing, was over, Susan said to her gently, 'Jane love, why don't you take your headache to bed? I'll bring you a cup of tea and some aspirin. Philip and I will wash up.'

Miss Gilmore gave her a grateful look, and said, 'Well, I think I shall, my dear, if you don't mind. Please don't worry—I'll be all right in the morning.'

Not liking it, Philip felt rather small.

He had never been in the kitchen before, and was taken aback by it. He had expected something like the rest of the house, with nothing post-dating 1935, but it was not like that at all. It was the kind of kitchen one sees in advertisements in colour magazines, all pine cupboards and red tiling, with a smart terracotta covering on the floor. A Rayburn stove burned where the old kitchen range had once stood, and there was also a modern electric cooker, with a split-level oven alongside it.

'This is very nice,' he remarked to Susan, who was piling the dishes in the stainless steel sink by the window. 'Sort of surprising,' he added.

'Oh, yes,' agreed Susan, as she squirted washing-up liquid, and turned on the tap. 'I'm sure it must be. You see, last year, a man came from the Electricity Board, and told Jane that if she didn't have the house rewired, it was going to burn to the ground. Not a comfortable thought, as she said at the time. So she sold all her mother's jewellery, and it was worth about five times as much as she expected. So we got the house rewired, and Jo got a new kitchen, having bellyached since 1938—I gathered—about the old one. She and Jane used to have the most hilarious arguments about whether there were cockroaches all over the floor, or not.'

'Were there?'

'Probably,' said Susan, giggling at a private memory. 'Jane wouldn't see a cockroach if it was sitting on her lap, wearing a fluorescent waistcoat. Anyway, Jo won. With the money that was left over, Jane had a new bathroom put in for herself behind her bedroom, and I got a new carpet, so everybody was satisfied. The cutlery goes in the drawer on the left, Philip, under the clock.'

Philip finished drying the dishes, and watched Susan making a pot of tea. She put it on a tray with a cup and saucer, a cream jug, and a bottle of aspirin. When she had taken it across the hall to Miss Gilmore's room, Philip went into the dining-room to wait for her, hoping that she would suggest watching some television. Once again, the portrait of Miss Gilmore's father seemed to demand his attention, and when Susan returned, she found him standing before the fireplace with his hands in his pockets, trying to outstare the old man across the room. Susan came and stood beside him on the hearth rug.

'Gruesome, isn't he?' she said.

Philip nodded.

'Terrible,' he agreed. 'I don't know how she can stand having him on the wall.'

Susan grinned.

'She can't get him off,' she explained. 'She has tried, but he's screwed on, and she thinks that if she pulled him off, the wall would come away with him. Mind you, I don't think she notices him as much as we do, and I suppose he's nothing like as bad as the real thing.'

'Was he our grandfather?' Philip wanted to know. He was hazy about generations.

'No. Great grandfather,' Susan told him. 'Our grand-father was Jane's eldest brother. He's been dead for a very long time.'

'What was his name?'

'Who? Old Sourface here, or our grandfather? Oh, well, it's the same, anyway. William Gilmore, of William Gilmore and Son, Limited, cookie makers to Her Royal Highness the Princess of Wales. Not this one, you know.

32

The last one. I forget which Queen she became.'

Philip looked mystified.

'Cookie makers?' he repeated. 'What on earth's cookie makers?'

'Makers of cookies,' said Susan impatiently, flopping into Miss Gilmore's armchair by the fire. 'You must know,' she went on, incredulously. 'They're everywhere. Gilmore's Chocolate Waffles, and Gilmore's Toffee Logs. They have them in our tuck shop, and I bet they have them in yours.'

Philip was astounded. He sat down opposite her, opened his eyes very wide, and said, 'Is that *them*? Do you mean my Mum's a Toffee Log Gilmore?'

'Descended from, I suppose,' replied Susan. 'The business was sold years ago, but the new people kept the name. I find it a bit embarrassing myself, and if you mention Toffee Logs to Jane, she goes green. She says the Gilmores are entirely to blame for people in the west of Scotland having the worst teeth in Europe.' She looked at Philip curiously, half laughing. 'Do you really mean you don't know any of this?' she asked.

Philip shook his head.

'No,' he assured her. 'I told you. My Dad went spare if anybody mentioned the Gilmores, and I'm only here now because of some rubbish about blood being thicker than water, and Mum not wanting me to stay with the Cawleys. She says they eat nothing but fish suppers, and I'd be up half the night watching video nasties. My Mum doesn't know what a video nasty is.'

'Oh, I see,' said Susan coolly. 'So she thought she'd make use of Jane.'

'I suppose so,' admitted Philip, uncomfortably. 'Did she say that?'

'Jane? No, she never would. She said, "Poor Margaret. I must try to help her out."'

Philip felt himself going red in the face. Like many fair people, he blushed easily. He made a last effort to defend himself, and his mother.

'She didn't even come to my Dad's funeral,' he muttered.

'Mum was upset. She should have come.'

'She was in bed with a bad back,' said Susan, icily now. 'She wanted to get up and go, but Jo and I wouldn't let her. There was snow on the ground, and she hadn't been out since before Christmas. But she was upset too. She said offence would be taken.'

Philip could see that he was not going to win this one, so he sensibly retreated.

'Well, but about him,' he said, jerking his thumb in the direction of his great grandfather's portrait. 'Why has he got that fancy chain round his neck?'

He sensed that Susan was glad that a quarrel had been averted.

'He was Lord Provost of Glasgow,' she said, unimpressed. 'He did pretty well out of Toffee Logs. Looking at him there, you'd never think his father began by selling cookies round Hillhead on a hand cart. The Victorians were great at rising in the world. Mind you, I've always wondered what he had to be so uppity about, but I suppose once a Princess took a fancy to his Logs, he was made.'

She gave her great grandfather a hostile look.

'Was he really as terrible as he seems?' asked Philip, who was finding all this fascinating. Gilmore's Chocolate Waffles, of which he was greedily fond, would never taste quite the same again.

'Yes, every bit,' replied Susan indignantly. 'He was hateful. He bullied his wife and sons, but it was Jane, who was the only daughter, who had the worst of it. She was at University when her mother died, and he made her give up her studies, and come home to keep house for him. She was pushed about like nobody's business. And it wasn't even necessary for her to be there. By that time our grandfather was married, and he and his wife were living here—he was in partnership with his father in the business, you see, because he was the oldest son. Our grandmother could have looked after the house, and let Jane off the hook. But the old man, who ruled the roost, said a mother's job was to look after her children—your

Mum and my Dad—and Jane could earn her keep by looking after the household. As if she needed to earn her keep at all! With her brains she could have taken a good degree, and got a job, and made something super of her life. Oh, it does make me so angry!' She stopped for a moment to regain her breath, then went on less vehemently, 'But that wasn't the worst of it. Jane had a boy friend—his name was Ewan MacNeill, and he lived two doors along the Avenue at *Winterwood*. He wanted Jane to marry him when she left school, but of course old Sourface wasn't having any of it. Then in 1939 the War began, and Ewan MacNeill was called up to the Army almost at once. He came home on leave in the spring of 1940, and asked Jane to get engaged to him, and she said she would. He was called back to join his unit sooner than he expected, and when he left her, he promised Jane that he would buy the engagement ring in London the next week, and send it to her. Only he didn't, and she never knew why. She never heard from him again, and he was killed at Dunkirk a few weeks later.'

'That was rotten,' said Philip, inadequately.

'Yes. After that, things went from bad to worse. Jane's second brother, Thomas, had emigrated to Australia in the early Thirties—to get away from his father, one gathers—then just after Ewan MacNeill was killed, her younger brother Hamish, whom she loved dearly, went to Canada and joined the Canadian Air Force. After the War, he settled in Canada. Your mother and my father grew up, and left home, then in the Sixties both our grandparents died. Jane was left here all alone with her father. He had a paralytic stroke, and was ill for years, but he lived till he was ninety. Before I came, Jane had been living by herself in this awful house for nearly ten years. I'm telling you, Philip, it would be enough to drive anybody batty. But she isn't. Not in the least.'

Philip looked inquisitively at his cousin's flushed, unhappy face.

'How do you know all this?' he asked her. 'Did she tell you?'

'God, no,' said Susan, appalled. 'She'd never talk about it. My Dad told me. He thinks she's fond of him, which is just like his cheek. She has a pretty good idea what makes him tick. She's not stupid.'

'What makes him tick?'

'Greed,' said Susan candidly. 'He calls it being business-like. When my Mum went off to America with one of the chaps from the Yacht Club, he realised that he'd have to send me home to school. So he totted it all up, and decided that it would be cheaper to send me to live with Jane, and go to day school, than it would be to send me to boarding school. Then he pretended he was doing it for Jane's sake, and that I'd be someone for her to be fond of. Like a puppy,' concluded Susan, with fierce bitterness.

'I think she is fond of you,' ventured Philip, sensing a deep sadness, but turning his eyes away from the bleak look on Susan's face.

But she shook her head.

'She tries very hard not to be,' she said. 'You see, I'm a Gilmore too, and what have Gilmores ever done but leave her in the lurch? Poor Jane, she just can't run the risk of being hurt again.'

7

A Strange Photograph

In spite of his determination that he would not become involved in the affairs of his great aunt Jane, the story which Susan had told him upset Philip, and that night he had trouble getting to sleep. It was not the sad story of Jane Gilmore's love affair that bothered him; Philip could not understand why people wanted to get married at all. It was the thought of all the family dying, or going away, until at last she was left alone with that frightening old man in the portrait. And even when he was dead, there had been no renewal of life for her; she had to go on living, year after year, all by herself in this great, gloomy house, in the loneliness that comes when voices fall silent, and love fails. No matter how often Philip told himself that it was her own fault for not packing her bags and leaving too, or that her father might not have been as bad as he seemed, or that we all have troubles, it was no good. Try as he might to forget, he saw again in his mind's eye that pale, abstracted face which had looked over his shoulder at the supper table, seeing—well, who could guess? And he wished that he had not had such unkind thoughts about her. Later on, of course, he would harden his heart again, but now, alone in the darkness, he was sorry.

And there was the matter also of that strange line of light, shining under the door of a room which was empty, and had had all its light bulbs removed. Philip thought that the uncanniness of it was just bearable because the mystery kept itself on its own side of the door, but it was a mystery nonetheless, which his visit with Susan had done nothing to solve. The previous afternoon, curiosity getting the better of fear, Philip had peeped round some of the other doors on the landing; each one opened on a heavily furnished, sumptuously curtained bedroom, with a tightly sealed window and an airless smell. The rooms were clean, swept and dusted, presumably, by the invisible Jo, but, although none had the suffocating nastiness of the purple room, they had a depressing feeling of abandonment and disuse. Which was not how the empty drawing-room felt. Just as he was at last dropping into sleep, Philip had a strange realisation of something which he had not noticed at the time, and of which he would not think again for some weeks to come. Although Miss Gilmore's father had been dead for twelve years, and although the room had stood forlornly empty for two, it did not feel as it appeared. Unlike the furnished bedrooms, it felt like a room that was inhabited, from which people had gone out only a few moments before.

In the morning, when Susan had gone off to the station with her hockey bag, Philip felt that he just had to get away from Wisteria Avenue for a while. He would go and visit his friends the Cawleys. Their house was as far as you could go from *The Mount,* even if it was only three quarters of a mile away. So he put on his jerkin, and came rattling downstairs as noisily as he could. In the hall, however, he had a thought; he ought to tell Miss Gilmore where he was going. This was something that his mother was very fussy about, and he saw her point.

She was sitting at the table in the dining-room, wearing a blue woollen dressing-gown over her high-collared white nightdress, drinking tea and glancing at the *Glasgow Herald* through half-moon spectacles. She turned her head, and, for once, did rest her eyes on Philip, giving him the grave but not unpleasant look which was probably the nearest she ever got to a smile.

'Hello,' she said.

'Aunt Jane,' said Philip, 'I'm going out. To see a friend, all right? Russell Cawley, his name is. He lives at Maxie Court, number 167.'

He was doubtful how much of this, if any, she had taken in, but she said, 'Yes. Good. Will you be back to lunch?'

Philip said that he would. Lunch at the Cawleys on a Saturday was a Scotch pie in your hand, eaten standing up, because everyone was in a rush to get away to Ibrox, to the football match. Mrs Cawley was hospitable, but she would not have counted him in when buying the pies.

Miss Gilmore nodded, and was returning her attention to the morning's news, when Philip, stung unaccustomedly in his conscience, thought to say gruffly, 'I hope your headache's better, Aunt Jane.'

Her reply bothered him.

'Oh, yes, thank you,' she said, and went on apologetically, 'I'm sorry about that. I do know how tiresome it is to have to sit at table with gloomy old persons, yet now I seem to have become one myself. I really am ashamed, but I just don't feel able to help it.'

Damn, Philip thought. She had noticed him giving her dirty looks after all. When he had thought her dark, heavy eyes were looking past him, they had actually been observing him all the time. However, he had the sense to see that the situation would not be improved by blundering apologies now, so he decided that he would make himself scarce, at once.

'Well, I'll be off now,' he said.

'Yes, all right, Philip—'

It was the first time she had actually called him by his name. He had wondered a few times whether she remembered it.

'What is it?' he asked.

'You might just call me Jane, if you don't mind. I don't feel at all auntly to you, and I'm sure you don't feel nephewly to me, so we'd be as well to drop the title, don't you think?'

For the life of him, Philip could not understand why he felt so pleased. But, 'Mum wouldn't approve,' he pointed out.

'Tough on her,' retorted Jane unexpectedly, and went back to reading the paper.

Philip grinned, and went off to fetch his bicycle.

It was marvellous to leave the dead air of the house

behind him, and go whizzing downhill on a sharp autumn morning, with cold air parting on either side of his body as he sliced through it. Soon there would be a frost, which would bring down the faded leaves, and blacken the dahlias in other people's gardens, but not yet. The city still perched obstinately on the edge of a beautiful summer, and later today there would be a mellow warmth in the sun.

From the top of the hill, Philip could see the grey line of the Clyde, with its great cranes and warehouses, and misty, blue-grey hills beyond. Half-way down, this view disappeared abruptly behind the rigid masses of sandstone tenements and modern office blocks. Philip crossed the main road at the traffic lights, and went weaving leisurely through the Park. On the other side, the road divided. On the left lay the private housing estate where his own home was, on the right the high Council flats where his friend Russell Cawley lived. Philip turned right, and cycled along the footpath to the tower block called Maxie Court, hoping that the lift would not be out of order. The Cawleys lived on the tenth floor.

But the lift went up smoothly, and, as usual, he was given a warm, easy welcome. It was a relief, after the draughty vastness of the house in Wisteria Avenue, to sit in the Cawleys' tiny, overheated living-room, with its draped net curtains and souvenirs of Tenerife, drinking Coke and watching with half an eye the continuous video show which the Cawleys provided. Philip accepted a lot of good-natured teasing from fat Mrs Cawley and her daughters about his posh auntie up the hill, and how they hadn't expected to see him, now that he had got so grand. Large, fair-haired Russell, as usual, said nothing except, 'Aw, shurrup, you lot. Ah'm tryin' tae watch this fillum.'

Afterwards, however, Philip felt that he had disappointed them by failing to make them laugh with stories of life at *The Mount*. He had, after all, promised last week to tell them all about it. But, for several reasons, he was not in the mood to joke about Jane, and he had no intention of telling the Cawleys that his great grandfather was Gilmore of Chocolate Waffle fame, and had once been Lord

Provost of Glasgow. As it was, they were always twitting him about being posh, although he knew, and they knew, that Russell's father, who was a bookmaker, earned ten times as much as Philip's father had ever earned at the Bank. Mrs Cawley said there was an extra pie, but Philip said he was expected back, and left. As he went down in the lift, he thought that after this encounter with normality, the house in Wisteria Avenue would seem stranger than ever. Had he but known it, the strangeness was only beginning.

Susan came home in the late afternoon, bringing the photographs, and they took them up to her room to look at them. Somehow, the delay in getting them had raised their expectation that they would be especially amusing, and consequently they examined them with a sense of anti-climax. At the beginning of the film, there had been some photographs taken by Susan at school last term, girls in blazers and summer frocks, standing in groups with their arms draped around one another's necks. The photographs taken in the empty room really were disappointing; they had not developed very clearly because of the red intrusion of the sun, and the poses which had seemed so hilarious at the time seemed less so now.

'I don't think you can send any of these to your Mum,' remarked Susan regretfully. 'She'll think I'm leading you astray.'

'That's what she says about Russ,' said Philip indifferently.

He was sitting on Susan's bed, shuffling the photographs, and thinking how silly the girls looked, when suddenly something else caught his attention. He didn't feel excited, he just noticed. Removing one of the prints from the pile, he looked at it more closely, and continued, 'Hey, look at this, though. One of us must have forgotten to wind the film on—we seem to have taken one on top of another. No, hang on—it's not that either.' But it was not till Susan had sat down beside him, and he heard her give a low

41

whistle of astonishment, that the real strangeness of what he was seeing sank in.

'Well, I'm damned,' he said.

It was the photograph of Philip doing his monkey impression, and he could be seen clearly enough, with his chin down on his chest, his legs bent, and his fingers scratching his armpits. But—not exactly behind him, but rather through him, could be seen a piece of furniture. It was a little blurred, but quite distinguishable, a kind of cabinet with cupboard doors on top, and drawers under-neath. It stood raised on four curved legs with carved claws for feet; the doors and drawers had brass handles, and there was a carved scroll along its top.

Susan and Philip looked at it for a long time in silence, then Philip said, a little hoarsely, 'Have we taken a photograph of something that isn't there?'

Susan didn't answer for a moment, but then, in a small voice, she replied, 'It's even queerer than that. Of course, it wasn't there when we took the photograph. Nothing was. But I know where it is. It's downstairs, in the sitting-room.'

Philip was doubtful.

'Are you sure?' he asked. 'I've never seen it.'

'You just mean you haven't noticed it,' Susan said. 'There's so much stuff in that room, you can't see anything properly. Jane calls it Gilmore's Repository. The cabinet's behind the door, with that green sofa in front of it, the one with tassels.'

Philip remembered the sofa. He had sat on it the day he arrived.

They sat speechless for a while, absorbing the strange-ness of this discovery, then Philip said tentatively, 'I suppose we might have a look—at the cabinet, I mean.'

Susan's brown face assumed an anxious look.

'Do you mean, look inside it?' she asked. 'I really wouldn't like to do that without asking Jane.'

Such scruples made Philip impatient.

'Why on earth not?' he demanded. 'You said yourself she didn't mind us poking about.'

'There's a difference,' Susan pointed out, 'between

42

wandering around the rooms of the house you live in, and rummaging in someone else's cupboards. You must see that.'

Philip did see, but it was inconvenient.

'Look,' he said. 'You can't ask her, unless you show her the photograph, and explain why you want to open the cabinet. She'll find it very peculiar, and you'll tie yourself in knots. I don't think that's a good idea.'

'Neither do I,' Susan agreed. 'It's so odd, it would probably worry her. Her headache's still bad, though she's pretending it isn't. Oh, dear. Perhaps we should forget the whole thing.'

'Oh, come on,' said Philip incredulously. 'You know we can't do that. This thing has happened, and in my opinion, we must follow it up. It isn't as if we're going to steal anything. And it's a sort of clue, isn't it?'

Susan eyed him uncertainly.

'Is it?' she asked. 'What to?'

'I don't know,' said Philip obstinately. 'All I know is that we went into that room because we saw a light that can't be explained shining under the door. We thought we hadn't found anything, didn't we? Well now, in a way, we have. It may only be something else that's impossible to explain, but there may be a connection. And I think we should investigate as far as we can, that's all.'

Susan slowly gathered up the photographs, straightened them, and tucked them away inside their paper folder.

'Yes. I expect you're right,' she said reluctantly.

When they had finished supper, Jane again went off to bed early. After they had washed up, Susan and Philip went into the sitting-room, and while Susan turned on the gas fire, Philip switched on the television, an automatic action of his. But neither he nor Susan sat down to watch the Saturday evening comedy programme; without a word, they pulled the sofa away from the cabinet and stood looking at it, perhaps both wishing, just a little, that Susan had made a mistake. But she had not.

43

'I don't like this,' she said.

Philip didn't ask what she didn't like, the fact of the cabinet's being there, or the prospect of going through its contents behind Jane's back.

'I'll look, if you don't want to,' he offered.

But Susan said, 'Oh, let's get on with it,' and turned a small gold key in the cupboard door. It swung silently open.

It all seemed very ordinary. In the cupboards, lined with dark blue paper, were wine glasses of every shape and size, just wine glasses, row upon row upon row. The top drawer contained table linen, folded into yellowing tissue paper. The middle one had sewing materials in it, a work basket, a button box, odd pieces of cloth and an embroidery frame.

'Not Jane's,' said Susan. 'She can't see well enough to sew.'

The bottom drawer seemed to be empty, apart from its lining of waxed paper, secured at the corners with drawing pins.

'Oh, hell,' said Susan, upset. 'I don't think I'd have minded quite so much if we had found something interesting, but now I've done something I don't approve of, and all for nothing.'

Philip was getting tired of this.

'I don't see any difference,' he told her bluntly. 'You can't say—'

'Oh, never mind,' interrupted Susan snappishly. 'Close the drawer, and for God's sake, turn that racket off. Poor Jane will be demented. Can't you ever think of anyone but yourself? Now we might as well give up the whole thing, and let the stupid light shine.'

Philip watched her as she threw herself petulantly into an armchair, flushed and pushing out her bottom lip. It was the first time he had seen her ruffled. He shrugged his shoulders, and bent down to push in the drawer.

And just as the inside, with its lining of blue, disappeared from view, he saw it—a tiny triangle of paper sticking out from under the lining, at one side. Hurriedly he wrenched the drawer open again, put in his finger, and tried to ease the triangle further out. Perversely it slid in the other direction, under the blue paper, and disappeared from view.

'Blast,' said Philip, under his breath.

But Susan heard him. Instantly, she was on her knees at his side.

'What is it? Have you found something?' she asked, eagerly.

'It's gone under the blue paper,' explained Philip, trying to sound cool. 'I think it's a post card, or an envelope. Let me get this pin out. There!'

He pulled out the rusty drawing-pin with his finger nails, turned back the lining paper, and removed a small buff envelope with its flap tucked in. They took it over to the fireplace to examine it, under the standard lamp.

The envelope contained one item only, a cutting from a very old newspaper. But it was remarkably fresh and clean, because it had not been exposed to the light. And perhaps it was this which made its contents seem so compelling, as if the event they told of had happened only yesterday.

Under the heading, 'KNIGHTSHILL MAN LOST AT DUNKIRK' were the words: 'We regret to report the death on active service of Pte Ewan MacNeill, 3rd Batallion, Royal Highland Fusiliers, serving in France with the British Expeditionary Force. Few details have yet been received, but it would appear that Pte MacNeill, having survived the hazards of the Allied retreat to Dunkirk, met his death under German shell-fire, while awaiting evacuation from the beaches.

'Ewan MacNeill, younger son of Mr and Mrs Albert MacNeill, *Winterwood*, 8 Wisteria Avenue, was a popular figure in local circles. A former pupil of Knightshill Academy, he was formerly employed in the offices of well-known city confectioners William Gilmore & Son, Ltd. He was an accomplished rugby and tennis player, who in 1938 and 1939 won the Doubles title of the West of Scotland Cup Competition, with his close friend, Hamish Gilmore. The sincere sympathy of the community will be extended to Mr and Mrs MacNeill, Ronald and Sarah, in their tragic loss.'

Philip read the words once, and Susan twice. Then she slowly put the cutting back in its envelope.

'Poor Jane,' she said sadly. 'She was only nineteen, and this is all that was left. I wonder who extended sympathy to her?'

8

Sunday

Strange things always seem stranger after nightfall than they do in the clear light of day. For the second night in succession, Philip slept badly. Tossing about in bed, tangled hotly with his duvet, he heard the clock of St Kentigern's strike eleven, twelve, one, two and three, before at last he fell into an uneasy sleep. Then he dreamed of cabinets with drawers full of Toffee Logs and Chocolate Waffles, and his great grandfather climbing out of his frame to stop him eating them. Then he heard the chill, monitory wail of an air raid siren, and he was lying on a beach, face downward in the sand, while shells went whistling over his head. About seven o'clock, he at last fell into normal sleep, and didn't wake till after ten. It was a relief to find that Susan had overslept after a bad night too; she told him so when he met her coming up from the bathroom, as he was going down.

Susan fried some bacon and eggs, and made toast. They managed breakfast for themselves at weekends. While they were eating, with the reproachful din of Presbyterian church bells in their ears, Jane came into the dining-room, wearing her overcoat and carrying her handbag.

'Church?' enquired Susan cheekily, spreading astonishment over her mobile face.

Jane chose to ignore this.

'Lunch,' she said. 'I forgot to tell you. Molly Watkins rang up on Friday. There's food in the larder, and I'll be back in the afternoon.'

'Cross at the green man,' Susan warned her, through a mouthful of egg.

Jane went out into the hall, and they could hear her

47

unlocking the stained glass inner door of the vestibule, then the heavy outer one. But instead of going out, she came back, and called, 'Susan! Bring me that book Scott Watkins lent me, will you? It's on the floor by the fireplace.'

Susan got up and went to fetch the book. As she passed the table, Philip squinted inquisitively at the title, wondering what kind of books old ladies read. It was *Advanced Nuclear Reactor Theory* by James Scott Watkins.

'Good Lord,' he said in amazement to Susan, when she returned. 'Can she understand that kind of stuff?'

'Oh, yes,' Susan assured him calmly, as she stretched for another piece of toast. 'She's a clever old thing. It was *Laser Physics* last week. She would have been a scientist, if someone else hadn't had other ideas.'

On impulse, Philip got up from the table, hurried out of the house, and sprinted down the leafy tunnel to the gate. Jane was still there; the gate had got stuck, and she was having difficulty getting out. Philip vaulted neatly over, and opened it for her from the outside.

'Hey, Jane,' he said. 'I need to know. Are you actually planning to blow us all up?'

Once again, her dark eyes regarded him reflectively, and he saw what Susan meant when she said that Jane could be amused, but didn't laugh with you.

'I could, if I put my mind to it,' she said. 'So watch it.'

With which she walked away down Wisteria Avenue in the sunshine.

'Who's James Scott Watkins?' Philip asked Susan, when he got back to the breakfast table.

'He's a Professor of Physics at the University,' Susan told him. 'He's nice. He and Jane were students together, away back in nineteen oatcake, and they're still good friends. She doesn't give him an inch, though—she checks all his calculations in that red notebook she keeps on the little table, and gives him hell if she doesn't agree with him. She's read a terrific amount, and he told me once that she's far brighter than he is.'

She gave her great grandfather one of the malevolent glances which never seemed to disturb him unduly, and began to clear the table. Philip followed her into the kitchen, intending to dry the dishes for her. Being cheeky to Jane had made him feel cheerful, and he said vigorously, 'Well now, what are we going to do today? Any ideas?'

He supposed that Susan would at least want to talk about the strange events of yesterday, to look at the uncanny photograph again, and discuss what, if anything, they might do next. He had had a few thoughts, during his sleepless hours, which he very much wanted to share with her. But he received a check.

'You can do what you like,' Susan replied firmly. 'I'm afraid I have my homework to do.'

'Oh, come on,' said Philip impatiently. 'You can do that later.'

'No, sorry, I can't,' said Susan. 'It always takes me most of Sunday. You wouldn't believe what I have to get through. Sometimes I think at our school they expect us to work harder at home than we do there. I've got nine bits of written work to do for tomorrow, and poetry to learn.'

Disappointment made Philip truculent.

'My Dad didn't approve of fee-paying schools,' he said. 'My Dad said they just produce people who think they're a cut above other people, for no reason. Stupid people, as often as not.'

It was odd, really. Philip had never got on well with his father, and had gone against everything for which his father stood. Yet he parroted his prejudices as if they were gospel truth.

Susan put the dirty dishes in the sink, and poured hot water over them. Then she turned round and faced Philip, with a none too pleasant expression on her dark face.

'It may interest you to know,' she said, 'that I agree with him. Not about producing people who think they're a cut above other people, although I suppose there could be a few silly enough to feel like that. However, I don't know any, and most of the people at school with me seem reasonably intelligent. But then, I agree with Jane, that most

49

people are intelligent, it's other things that are wrong. And she agrees with me that the best schools should be there for everybody, without paying—at least for everybody who'll use the opportunities they offer. I suppose they'd be wasted on people like you, with your *Beanos* and your everlasting telly. Look, Philip—I know it's a rotten, unfair world, but I can't help to change it until I'm grown up, and I'll be able to do it better if I get a good education first. People of your sort never help to change the world, they just bellyache about it being the way it is. So don't try to put me off my work—I'm not Russ Cawley, you know.'

Philip was so taken aback that he couldn't think of a word to say. Scarlet with mortification, he walked out of the kitchen, through the dining-room, and out of the house. Hardly noticing where he was going, he went along a mossy path in front of the sitting-room window, and round the corner into the garden at the side of the house. There he found a little stone bench, and sat down to be furious alone.

It was his own fault, he told himself, when the first fog of anger had begun to clear from his mind. He should have done what he had meant to do, and kept his distance. He had known that she would be snobby and stroppy, yet he had allowed himself to be disarmed, because it had suited her, for a while, to pretend to be nice. He should have remembered that she was Alex Gilmore's daughter, and his Dad had had plenty to say about Alex Gilmore, big, boastful and good looking, with his sports car and his job in the oil business, sneering at Alan North because he had to travel on the bus, and work as a teller at the Clydesdale Bank, Bishopbriggs. However critical she might pretend to be of her father, of course Susan Gilmore would despise anyone called North.

Philip got up, and paced up and down, kicking at the grass and weeds until his trainers and the bottoms of his cords were soaking wet. He hardly noticed, as grievances crowded to his mind like wasps to bruised fruit.

It was the remark about the *Beano* and the telly which hurt most. OK, he liked the *Beano* and the telly, what was wrong with that? Philip had never worked at school, preferring to lark about with Russ and the other boys; it had irritated his father fearfully, because, even if he had not approved of fee-paying schools, he had approved of school. Philip knew that teachers thought he was stupid, but he had never cared what teachers thought, and he did not regard himself as stupid. 'I could do it if I liked,' he had always told himself. 'If I was a swot, like Specky Delaney, or Timothy Green.' But to be told to his face, and by a girl, that good schooling would be wasted on people like him ... She was a mean bitch, and he would never speak to her again.

As his anger gradually cooled into a sense of wounded self-righteousness, Philip left the little stone seat, and began to move, for no particular reason, round to the back of the house. It was heavy going. Sometimes up to his chest in nettles and grass, he pushed on through the ruined kitchen garden; here arthritic trees, too old ever to bear fruit again, thrust out gnarled arms over a tangle of bramble and raspberry canes which it would have needed a bulldozer to clear. The rear wall of the house heaved its enormous shadow over the ground, and it was dank, sunless and cold. Philip was glad when, pushing open a peeling green door in a wall, he found himself in sunshine again. Here was the rose garden, with its derelict swing and empty lily pond, which he and Susan had seen from the mysterious first floor room. He glanced up, almost afraid of seeing a face looking out, but the dark windows kept their secret, whatever it was.

Really wet now, and covered with prickly seeds and bits of grass, Philip thought that he would push on round to the front door as quickly as he could, and go upstairs to change. But, as he was trying to find some trace of a path, he caught sight of the little stone building which he had seen from the window, in the corner of the garden. Suddenly curious, he waded through the soaking grass towards it.

It was at once obvious that no one had come here for years. The building was, as Susan had supposed, a summer house, a stone version of the chalet which is more often made of wood. Its windows were cracked and draped with cobwebs, embroidered this autumn morning with pin-head drops of silver dew; its door, when Philip gently pulled it open, swung out loosely on one fragile hinge. Not liking it, but wanting to know what was there, he trampled down the encircling vegetation and stepped inside.

There was a lot of ancient junk, a rusty hand mower, croquet mallets, faded deck chairs, a punctured, perishing rubber ball. The smell was awful, damp and unwholesome; the whole place had the feel and the reek of desolation and neglect. Philip was just about to back away when he caught sight of a garden bench, a smaller version of the kind you see in public parks, half concealed by a pile of mouldy cushions. He never knew why he pulled the cushions away, never knew what extra sense made him look down at the slatted seat, but he did, and saw letters roughly carved out of the shabby green paint. 'E.M. J.G. 31 MAR 40.' He did not have to wonder whose initials these were. And although Philip was not a person who had ever cared much for the pain of others, some tiny holes had appeared recently in the armour of his selfishness, so that he felt a faint stirring of pity for the young man who had only eight more weeks to live, and for the pale old woman who had lived all her life without husband or children, and had forgotten how to smile.

It was while he was putting the cushions back, because, if he did not, the door would not close, that Philip noticed something shiny at his feet. The stone floor of the summer house had been covered with wooden planks; rotted now, they had warped and stretched and sprung back from their holding nails, so that Philip was able to put his fingers into a gap. He pulled out a small, oval object which he recognised as half of a gold locket. His mother had a whole one, two ovals of gold which opened like a book on a tiny hinge to show two photographs—Mrs North's had one of her husband, and one of Philip as a small child. What he now held was one half of such an ornament, the half without the little gold loop through which you could pass a chain. Philip could see that it had the remains of a photograph in it, but water had seeped behind the glass, destroying the image. There was no knowing now whose picture it had been, or how it got here; some careless Gilmore woman had let it slip from her fingers, he supposed, and it had gone beyond reach between floor-boards which were then firmly nailed down. Philip put it in his pocket, and turned back towards the house. He would keep it, he thought. No one could possibly want such a thing now; probably its owner was long since dead. Perhaps he could sell it; he had heard that even small pieces of gold were valuable. What he would not do was to show it to Susan, or tell her about the carved initials on the bench. He would never tell her anything, ever again.

9

Philip's Theory

When he went indoors, Philip fetched himself an enormous slice of ham and egg pie, some plums and a glass of orange juice from the larder, and took them up to his room. Occasionally, as he ate, he could hear Susan moving about next door, as she got up to fetch a book, or put something in her school bag. But she did not come in.

After he had finished his lunch, and changed into clean clothes, Philip forced himself to sit down with pen and paper, and write a letter to his mother. He found it difficult. Apart from his problems with spelling and punctuation, very little had happened which he could possibly tell his mother in a letter. It became the 'I am fine, I hope you are fine' type of letter, as dull as ditchwater—but it would have to do. After he had put it into one of the envelopes which his mother had stamped and addressed for him before he left home, he lay on the bed and read an old *Beano,* but with a bitter feeling which took away all the pleasure. At five o'clock, Susan put her head round the door.

'Get lost,' said Philip emphatically, before she had time to speak. 'Just get lost.'

He rolled over on the bed so that his back was towards Susan, and lay there stiffly, waiting for her to withdraw. But of course, being impervious to snubs, she did not. She came in, and sat down on the end of the bed.

'Don't be cross, Philip,' she pleaded. 'Please. I've come to apologise.'

'I don't want you to apologise,' growled Philip. 'I just want you to get out of here.'

'Oh, Philip! Don't be so huffy.' She put a hand on his foot, but he kicked it off angrily. 'You started it, you know, trying to provoke me about private schools. But I shouldn't have said what I did. It was foul of me, and I am sorry, honestly.'

It was handsome, but Philip had no intention of giving in yet. He kept silent for a moment, then he said coldly, still looking at the wall, 'It isn't very nice to be told you're stupid, you know.'

'Oh, damn,' said Susan. 'You're not making this easy, are you? I didn't say you were stupid.'

'You did.'

'Sorry, I did not. What I said was that you waste your time. If you were stupid, that wouldn't matter, but you're so obviously very intelligent, it just seems a pity to me that you can't find anything better to read than comics.'

Philip flounced round, scowling, on the bed.

'Like what?' he demanded. '*Advanced Nuclear Reactor Theory,* I suppose.'

Susan laughed, and pushed him over on his back.

'You might start with something a bit more basic,' she said. 'But yes, eventually, if you were interested. Why not?'

Totally against his intention, Philip felt flattered, and he warmed to her again. But then he checked himself, and said, 'It's no business of yours, what I read.'

'No,' agreed Susan wearily. 'I know it isn't. Read your blinking *Beanos,* then. But let's be friends again, Philip. *Please.*'

Philip could not hold out against this, or against her genuinely contrite face.

'OK,' he said gruffly. 'But just mind what you're saying, in future.'

'I shall,' promised Susan meekly.

For a while, at least, a friendship is always cosier after the making up of a quarrel, and so this one proved. Later that night, when they were both sitting in Susan's room, drinking hot chocolate which Susan had brought upstairs in a Thermos jug, Philip, who was once again looking through the folder of photographs, said, 'Look, Sue. In this photograph—the one of me with my head up the chimney—you can see a bit of something at the side of the fireplace. A table, I think.'

Susan came and knelt down beside the corduroy bean bag, where Philip was sprawling, with his mug of chocolate on the tiny hearth beside him. She looked carefully where his finger was pointing, and saw that there was indeed a table leg, and a thin sliver of table top.

'Clever you,' she said.

Philip was pleased. He had a theory, worked out in the hot dark hours of last night, and the photographed slice of table strengthened it considerably. He had meant to try it on Susan in the morning, and, since they were friends again, saw no reason why he should not do so now.

'Listen,' he said. 'I've got an idea. I've been wondering— do you suppose there's any reason why one—or one and a bit—of these photographs might show furniture, and the others not?'

'You're the one with the idea,' Susan pointed out.

'OK, then,' said Philip eagerly, picking up the photographs which showed the cabinet and the table. 'These two are the only ones taken with the camera actually pointing at the wall, aren't they? This one'—he fanned out the remaining prints on the rug—'of you standing on your hands, and this one of you doing the Dance of the Dying Swan—oh, and this one of me, imitating Hitler—were all taken in the middle of the floor, with no particular background. Now, what I wonder is—if you take a photo with the camera pointing straight at the wall, is it just possible that it will photograph pieces of furniture which used to stand there, and now don't?'

Susan thought about this, and Philip could see admiration for his idea, and amazement at the possibility of its being true, struggling for expression on her face.

'Yes,' she said eventually. 'Of course, I'm sure you're right. Do you remember, all round the room there were marks on the walls, where the furniture used to be. Gosh.'

'Sue,' said Philip, 'where did you buy that camera?'

Susan laughed, but not whole-heartedly.

'I didn't buy it,' she told him. 'Jane gave it to me. She found it in a cupboard—it was my Dad's, when he was a kid. Jane says he was a perfect menace, rushing around photographing everybody when they least wanted to be photographed.'

'Do you suppose he photographed the old man?' asked Philip, overawed by the thought of such boldness.

'I think that was what she was implying,' said Susan. 'One of these days I'm going to have to lash out on a new model. It's getting difficult to find films, it's so antique. Fortunately Mr Rushasnap down the road still has a supply.'

'Can you get one tomorrow?' enquired Philip. 'We could try out my theory after school.'

'Yes, all right. Philip.'

'Mn?'

'When I came upstairs tonight, I saw the light again, under the door. What I wonder is—do you think it's there when we're not looking at it?'

Philip looked at her in surprise, then he laughed.

'Oh, come on, Sue,' he said. 'That's impossible to answer. Think about it.'

But it was an important question, nonetheless.

Later on, as he was making a pile of his dirty clothes, because Susan had told him that Jo came to do the washing on Monday, Philip found, in the pocket of his jeans, the piece of gold locket which he had picked up that morning in the summer house. He had forgotten about it. Now he stood in his pyjamas, looking at it, a slightly scratched, dented frame containing a small, ruined scrap of photograph. You could see where the pin had fallen out of the tiny hinge, allowing this part to detach itself from the other. Philip turned the thing over in his fingers, and wondered whether to show it to Susan, now that they were on good terms again. But he decided not to. It would be a little punishment for her rudeness about his reading habits. He had forgiven her, but a small wound still stung.

Oddly, it was Jane, who seemed to have a gift for the unexpected, who laid a touch of healing on this sore place. One evening, later in the week, when Philip went down for supper at half-past six, he found the table unlaid, and Jane in the kitchen, in her apron, opening a large tin of baked beans.

'Nothing is ready,' she informed him, 'and it's all your fault.'

'My fault?' said Philip, amazed. 'How so?'

'Well,' said Jane, sloshing the beans hastily into a pan, and putting it on the stove, 'I went upstairs at two o'clock to put in a clean towel for you, and spent most of the afternoon reading your *Beanos*. I don't know what happened to Eggo the Ostrich, but I'm relieved to see they still have Lord Snooty. It gives me a sense of security in a changing world. Lay the table for me, there's a good boy.'

10

Maps, a Desk and a Painting

On Monday afternoon, Susan was putting a new roll of film into her camera when Philip arrived in her room, carrying another, much more up-to-date camera.

'What's that for?' Susan asked.

'It's for an experiment,' Philip explained. He put down his school bag on the floor, and laid the camera on Susan's desk. 'I've been thinking today about these queer photographs, and I can't help wondering —Sue, is it possible that it's the camera that's queer, not the room at all? Perhaps the camera's coming up with things it has taken before, as if it had a memory bank, like a computer, or something. If your Dad ran around snapping everything, like Jane said—'

'Yes, I do see what you mean,' agreed Susan. 'But that wouldn't explain the light under the door, Philip.'

Philip frowned. 'No, it wouldn't,' he said. 'I hadn't thought of that. Well, maybe they're both queer, the room and the camera. Anyway, I thought I'd check out the camera, so I've borrowed this one from Russ. He got it for his birthday last week, so it's split new. When you take the photographs today with your camera, I'll take the same things with this one. If yours come out with furniture on, and mine don't, it will prove that your camera is weird.'

'That's very clever,' said Susan approvingly. 'I told you you were bright. Come on, then.'

And they went downstairs to the empty room.

The day had been more overcast than of late, with a thin curtain of cloud drawn across the sun. Susan pointed out that it would be better for taking photographs than having sunshine spilling all over the floor. In the still grey light, they began to make their way round the walls, rather like people at an Exhibition, stopping at each darkened patch to examine it, and try to visualise the object which had once stood in front of it. There was, indeed, a low table-shape on the wall to the right of the fireplace, and, at the spot where Philip had been photographed as a monkey, the outline of the cabinet downstairs was perfectly recognisable.

'I can't think why I didn't notice it before,' Susan said, 'except that I wasn't looking at the marks particularly. I wonder why Jane kept it? Normally she doesn't care at all about possessions, for all that she has so many.'

'Sentimental value,' said Philip. 'That's what it's called. It's why my Mum keeps her Grandpa's desk. It takes up half our sitting-room, but she won't get rid of it. Says it's an heirloom. Daft, really.'

But Susan was no longer listening. She had gone back to studying the shapes on the walls.

'They're like maps, aren't they?' she asked presently. 'Only it isn't always easy to imagine the elevations. I mean, you can tell this was a sofa, because of the legs, and the sausage shapes where the arms were, but these rectangles could have been anything.'

Philip was glad that he knew what she was talking about; sometimes he lent half an ear to Geography lessons at school.

'With any luck, your camera will take the elevations,' he said.

'Yes. How many maps are there, Philip?'

'Twelve,' said Philip, after a quick count. 'That's including the cabinet and the small table.'

'Good,' said Susan. 'This film has ten exposures, and since we don't have to take these two again, that'll allow me to take everything.'

So they went round again, and every shape that Susan photographed with her old camera, Philip carefully took again with Russ's new one.

'I'll take the film to Mr Rushasnap on my way to the station in the morning,' said Susan, as they removed the spools, and sealed them up. 'I'll beg, implore and beseech him to have them ready for me after school, because I honestly don't think I could wait a moment longer. I'm a good customer, and he is called Rushasnap, after all.'

Mr Rushasnap obliged, less because Susan was a good customer than because she always enquired politely about the health of his wife and cat. She was late home next afternoon, because of her music lesson, but when she came bounding upstairs Philip could tell from the spring in her step that the experiment had been successful. She fell into his room, dropping her bags as she did so, and collapsed onto the bed, pushing two red and yellow envelopes under his nose.

'There now,' she gasped, triumphantly.

Philip switched on his bed lamp, tilted the shade, and held the photographs to the light. A glance at those taken with Russ's camera proved one point at least; it was Susan's camera that was freakish. The photographs which Philip had taken showed only what had been visible to the naked eye; patches of bare wall were revealed boringly as he flicked the prints over. Those taken with Susan's camera were a very different matter. With his lips pursed in a silent whistle of astonishment, Philip thumbed through them, then thumbed through them again.

They were not like photographs of completely solid objects. There was something slightly grey and vaporous about them, an indistinctness where the edges met the air. Yet every one showed a recognisable piece of furniture, a tall bookcase with glass doors, a bow-fronted chest of drawers with china bowls on top, a high-backed, tasselled sofa, larger than any of the ones downstairs.

'It's no wonder Jane sold that stuff,' remarked Susan, when she had got her breath back. 'It's far nicer than anything that's left here, even the cabinet. I just hope she got a decent price for it.'

But Philip was not really paying attention. A sudden, sharp exclamation from him brought Susan swiftly to look over his shoulder. He had taken one photograph from the pile, and was staring at it with an expression of disbelief on his face which Susan would have found comic, had it not also been so tantalising.

'What is it, then?' she asked impatiently.

It was a photograph showing a desk, a wide, leather-topped one with a space in the centre for one's knees, and on either side a stack of little drawers, with round wooden knobs.

'It's this,' said Philip, breathless, and stammering a little. 'It's—this desk, Sue. Jane didn't sell this. We've got it at home. It's been in our house for as long as I can remember.'

'What?' squealed Susan. 'Are you sure?'

'Of course I'm sure. I told you yesterday, but I don't suppose you were listening. Mum won't get rid of it. Sentimental value. She calls it Grandpa's desk. Crikey. I've never thought about it before, but of course—old Sourface downstairs must have been my Mum's grandpa.'

'Good God,' exclaimed Susan, pulling a face. 'Fancy calling him anything as human as Grandpa. Well, this is a new development, and no mistake.'

She stood frowning, in silence, as Philip put all the photographs back in their folders, nor did Philip, who felt really shaken, have anything else to say. But then, typically, Susan had a change of mood.

'Ah, well,' she said, 'we must talk about it later. But let's go down to supper now, for goodness' sake. It's Goulash with Dumplings, the smell is gorgeous, and I'm absolutely starving.'

By an odd coincidence—perhaps—when they arrived in the dining-room, the children found Jane standing in front of the oil painting of a stag being devoured by hounds. She was contemplating it with a fastidious expression on her well-bred face.

'I was wondering,' she remarked to Susan, 'whether anyone might be insane enough to want to buy this. I read in the *Herald* that the brute who painted it is enjoying a revival—if enjoying is the right word. The rates are due at the end of next month, and something will have to go.'

'I can't believe anyone is as insane as all that,' said Susan candidly, then added, somewhat daringly, 'I'll tell you what, though. There's a nice cabinet behind the door in the Repository. Why don't you sell that?'

'It's a fake, unfortunately,' said Jane ruefully. 'Not worth the trouble of selling—I need five times what it would fetch. Still, never mind. There's quite a lot of silver left, if I can remember where to look for it.'

And so one, very minor, mystery was solved.

There were times, throughout the weeks when these strange events were occurring, when Philip did things without really knowing why. Sometimes their significance was only slight, as when he had found the initials on the bench in the summer house, sometimes it was great, as was to prove the case with the task he set himself that evening. But each time, he acted on impulse, and without thought. Afterwards, it seemed odd that he should have done so, but only mildly odd in the midst of so many oddnesses.

After supper, while Susan was doing her homework, and having her bath, Philip got a large sheet of paper, which he tacked to the floor in his bedroom. Then he fetched the ghostly photographs, pencil, rubber and Susan's water colour paintbox. When Susan came upstairs from the bathroom, she found him busy making a picture of the old drawing-room downstairs.

'I'm just curious to know what it looked like when it was furnished,' he told her, although she had not asked him why he was doing it.

Susan stood for a while watching him, rubbing her wet head with a towel, until her short hair stood up in black spikes all over it.

'That's very good,' she said, approvingly.

Philip had painted the room as they had seen it from the door, with the window at the far end, and the fireplace on the right. He had made the walls, carpet and hearth rug vaguely fawn and brown, but had defined the furniture much more robustly. Susan instantly recognised the cabinet, the bookcase, the chest of drawers and the desk, standing in their correct places around the walls. More tentatively, Philip had sketched in on either side of the fireplace cushioned chairs, in the same design as the sofa, and had allowed himself a limited exercise of imagination, by putting a clock and vases on the chimney piece, and a bowl of fruit on the table beside the fire.

'It needs pictures,' he said, sitting back on his heels, and beginning to rinse out his brushes. 'There must have been some. Did you notice any maps of pictures, Sue?'

Susan shook her head.

'I wasn't looking,' she admitted. 'But there certainly were some. Jane sold them, along with the furniture. I suppose they must have been better than those monstrosities downstairs.'

Philip got up from the floor, eyeing her speculatively.

'Is there any chance of getting another film for your camera tomorrow?' he said. 'I'll pay for it this time. I wouldn't half like to see what the pictures were.'

Uncanny as it was, it had become a game to him now, and he was surprised to discover that Susan did not see it in quite the same way.

She said, 'No. Actually, Philip, I don't think we should take any more photographs with that camera.'

'Why not?' asked Philip.

Susan sat down, and gave him a darkly serious look which reminded him of Jane.

'I've got the jitters,' she confessed. 'I was thinking about it in the bath. You see—Jane didn't say that my Dad ran around snapping furniture, she said he ran around snapping people. I'd absolutely hate it if we photographed someone who'd been dead for years, and let's face it, apart from Jane, everyone who lived here when our parents were kids *has* been dead for years. Furniture is one thing, but I think we should keep people out of this. Do you understand what I mean, Philip?'

Philip thought that he did, but would perhaps have taken the risk, until he thought of Jane's old father. Then he decided that he agreed with Susan.

'All right,' he said. 'If that's how you feel. I'll think of some other way to put pictures in my painting. I'm going to bed now. That's ten striking, and I'm shattered.'

Susan said good night, in evident relief, and went away. Then, just as Philip had climbed under his duvet, and was about to switch off the light, she reappeared.

'Philip,' she said, sitting down hard on his feet, 'I've been thinking.'

'Oh, God,' groaned Philip, yanking out his feet from under her behind. 'What about now?'

'About that desk you were telling me about—the one in your sitting-room,' said Susan. 'I wonder whether we ought to go over to your house, and have a look at it. I mean, it does seem like a lead, doesn't it?'

'How does it?'

'Well—we did find the newspaper cutting about Ewan MacNeill in the cabinet, didn't we? Perhaps there might be another clue in the desk.'

'But another clue to what?' Philip asked. He was tired, and beginning to be difficult. 'Clues have to lead to something. What does this lead to? What are we looking for?'

Susan didn't know either. But Philip had been obstinate when she had not wanted to open the cabinet, and she was equally obstinate now.

'All I can tell you,' she said, 'is that I have the strongest feeling that all this must mean something— the light under the door, the photographs, the press cutting—and now this business of the desk's being at your house. They're all part of the same puzzle, and if we had a few more parts, a pattern might begin to emerge. Do you have a key to your place?'

Lord, Philip thought. Women were persistent. 'No,' he said. 'Mrs Balloch next door has it. I could get it, I suppose.'

Just as it was Susan's turn to be obstinate, now it was his turn to feel reluctant, and he could not easily explain. All he knew was that he did not want to return, without his

65

mother, to that empty house, to the sitting-room where his father had lain, bird-faced on the sofa, all through the last summer of his life, listlessly watching television, with a neglected cup of tea on the table beside him. The desk was in that room too, uneasy in the company of teak coffee tables and a tweed-covered three piece suite.

'I don't know that there's much point,' he said. 'Mum's such a ferocious spring cleaner, I'm sure she'd have found anything that was to be found. Anyway, one of the drawers doesn't open. It never has. Somebody must have locked it, and lost the key.'

'Well, honestly! Haven't you Norths ever heard of picking locks?' demanded Susan, indignantly.

'Yes, of course,' replied Philip, with impatience. 'But the stupid thing won't be picked. And Dad wouldn't force it, in case he split the wood. He said it would be vandalism, because the desk is worth a lot of money. Besides, Mum reckons there'll be nothing important in it.'

Susan was aghast at such lack of imagination.

'I'd have to find out, if the desk was mine,' she said severely.

'Ah, yes,' teased Philip, heaving her off the bed with his foot, and pulling up the duvet, 'but we're not all as nosy as you, are we?'

Before Susan departed, however, it was agreed that they could not go to Philip's house until the weekend, even if they wanted to. For the rest of the week, one or both of them had late activities after school, and, by the time they got home, it was almost dark. To Philip's relief, the matter would have to be shelved till Saturday. What they did not know, at this point, was that before Saturday they would be, once again, in a state of war.

11

Squally Weather

Towards the end of the week, the weather changed completely. During the early hours of Friday morning, the wind rose wildly, and several times in the night the children woke, disturbed by the rattling of tiles, the drumming of rain on skylights, the sobbing of the gale around the roof. At eight o'clock, Susan went off to school in her brown waterproof and wellingtons, scowling into the wind with its burden of wet leaves; Philip, who left later, had to pedal downhill against the storm, his cagoule blowing out around him like an orange balloon. Cars and buses had their lights on, and their tyres swished smoothly over the black, shiny surface of the street. It was the kind of morning which warns churlishly that winter is to come.

At school, Philip had a bad day. Before break, he had spilt glue on Mary Fyne's embroidery, and painted spectacles on Russ with green paint, while Mr Grainger was out of the room, answering the telephone. By lunch time, he had got all his sums wrong, and had scored two out of fifteen in a history test. At lunch time, when the weather had eased up temporarily, he broke bounds, and, at Russ's suggestion, went down on the railway line. They were seen by a teacher coming back from lunch in town, and at two o'clock they were summoned to the headmaster's room. Mr Tilling did not rant and rave; he was not that type. But he did tell them that he would not be responsible for fools who could not obey rules made for their own safety, and added that, but for the situation of Philip's mother, he would suspend them both until Christmas. Instead, they were forbidden to play football for the school until further notice, and were sentenced to two weeks' litter duty, which meant that they must spend breaks trailing around the playground with plastic dustbin liners, picking up potato crisp bags and orange peel which other people dropped in order to give them work to do.

Philip cycled back to Wisteria Avenue in the rain, cold and angry and miserable, his misery made worse by a sensation which was unusual, unwelcome, and quite impossible to explain. He felt that he had let Jane down. Not his mother, or his dead father, or Susan, whose reproachful faces seemed to float in front of his eyes as he pedalled up Cliff Road into the gale, but Jane, the least judgemental person in the world, who fed him and made his bed, but hardly ever spoke to him, and who, he was convinced, hardly noticed that he was there. And why, he wondered bitterly, as he kicked the front gate wildly open, did that thought also give him so much pain?

Susan, arriving shortly afterwards, made the innocent mistake of saying, 'Hello! You're back early, aren't you? I thought you were going to indoor football training?' She was sent on her way with a force that could not have been ruder, if all Philip's troubles had been her fault.

The next week was a dreadful one. All weekend, Philip was out at the Cawleys', wallowing in their sympathy and indignation against Mr Tilling, who was so out of touch with the modern world that he punished laddies for behaving in a normal way. So said the Cawleys. Back at Wisteria Avenue in the evening, Philip found neither sympathy nor censure, since neither Jane nor Susan understood what the trouble was. However, as was his custom, Philip tried to work out his own anger on those who happened to be around at the time, and was not helped at all by the awareness that he was being thoroughly mean and unfair.

He had had a lot of practice in similar situations at home. He slouched down to meals, said neither 'Please,' nor 'Thank you,' at the table, and indicated without words that he disliked everything that was placed in front of him. He failed to wipe his feet when he came into the hall, refused to help with the washing-up, and spent all his free time in the sitting-room, sprawling in front of the television, which had been an unwanted Christmas gift to Jane from Susan's father. Every ten minutes he got up, and turned the volume up louder. After a few kindly attempts to find out what was causing all this, Susan, tired of being snarled at, went her own way; Jane, from the beginning, had paid no attention, although from time to time Philip caught an expression in her eyes which he could not read, but which did not improve his mood in the slightest.

Things came to a head on Friday evening, a whole week after the incident at school, when Philip spilled red-currant jelly on the table cloth; Susan was watching him, and was sure that he had done it on purpose. She controlled herself until Jane had left the room, then she lost her temper completely.

'Now, listen, you,' she began, her face turning a dull, ugly red with long-suppressed fury, 'I reckon we've had just enough of you, with your rotten manners and your slobby behaviour. You put that jelly on the cloth on purpose, you dirty little pig.'

'I didn't.'

'You did. I saw you. Have you any idea how long it takes poor Jo to wash and iron cloths like these, or are you so used to being waited on hand and foot by your adoring mother that you don't give a damn how much work you make for anyone else? It would take a mother to love you—'

'Just a minute—'

'No!' shouted Susan, thumping the table with her brown fist. 'Don't you "Just a minute" me. For once, you can shut up, and listen. You're a spoilt brat, that's what you are. I suppose you've been in trouble at school again—certainly Jane and I haven't done anything to put your ugly face out of order—and now you're taking it out on us. Well, don't bother. We need you like we need a filthy winter, and we've seen it all before. You're a typical Gilmore male, you are, never pleasant unless you're getting all your own way, and not always then. You're like my father, and you're exactly like old Sourface there—my God, you even look like him. I've noticed it before, and it gives me the heebie-jeebies. I wouldn't like to be your daughter, when you grow up.'

They had both risen to their feet, and before Philip could think of a word to say in reply, or do the unforgivable by punching a girl in the teeth, Susan seized him furiously by the shoulders, whirling him round with unexpected strength to confront the portrait of his great grandfather. Then she burst into tears and ran out of the room; her footsteps thudded in his mind as she pounded away upstairs, and he heard the distant bang of her bedroom door like a clout on his ear.

Philip stood alone in the middle of the dining-room. No one had ever spoken to him like that in his life. He looked up into the arrogant, belligerent face of old William Gilmore, and in a devastating instant, he saw that it was true. At home, often and often, when he was sulking in the bathroom after a row, he had seen his face in the mirror, looking just like that, angry, self-righteous, with hard blue eyes. The fury began to ebb out of Philip, leaving him tremulous and sick. He groped for a chair, and sat down.

Jane came in, but did not speak to him. She fetched a tray, and took the dirty dishes out into the kitchen to wash up. Philip could hear the clatter of cutlery against the sink. When he felt that his legs had stopped shaking, at least enough to allow him to climb the stair, he went up silently, and shut himself in his room. He knew that this time Susan would not come in to apologise, so, after a little while, he went to bed. Too upset to read, he lay with the light on, going over and over in his mind the terrible words which Susan had spoken to him downstairs, seeing with his inner eye that terrible old man's face as the reflection of his own. And in the emptiness which he had become, he acknowledged that what Susan had said was true.

He had behaved abominably. Susan was right about that, and right, too, that nothing had been her fault, or Jane's. Yet he had made them suffer, as he made his mother suffer, when she was not in the wrong either. He had put the jelly on the cloth on purpose; it was the sort of thing he

70

did, occasionally, not knowing why, except that there was pleasure in annoying, when you had been annoyed. At home, he would break a saucer, or scratch the paint on the kitchen door. Petty vandalism, his father had called it. When he was little, they had smacked him, now his mother shouted at him. He didn't mind either very much. Only—did it make him more like Gilmore males? Greedy and irresponsible were the words Susan had used of her father, even if she had also said he could be fun to be with. Only pleasant when they were getting all their own way. All of which was bad enough—but not as bad as being compared to the heartless old man who had bullied Jane, and spoiled her life.

Philip lay on his back, with every drop of anger drained out of him. He could not understand the way he felt, for usually, after any quarrel, a steely belief in his own rightness kept him from considering the point of view of other people. But tonight, he did not feel like that. He had lived for only a few weeks in this house, with a tired old woman and a young girl who loved her, but they had changed him, he did not know how. Life with his father had given Philip a poor opinion of women, and he had come here comfortably believing that these two were selfish snobs whom he would have to put up with for a few weeks, and might then forget. But instead, because they really cared about other people, over and over again they had unintentionally shamed him. Philip remembered what Jane had said, when his mother had wanted to dump him on her, after years of neglecting her—'Poor Margaret, I must try to help her out.' He remembered how Jane, who was not supposed to know how to look after children, cooked delicious meals, and made the most marvellous packed lunches, when it was obvious most of the time that she was too unwell to bear the sight or the smell of food. He remembered that she had not come to his father's funeral because she had a bad back, and that all the unkind things his mother had said, about her telling lies and making feeble excuses, were untrue. And he remembered that she liked comics, and thought that the best schools should be

71

for everyone. Then there was Susan, who had insisted that Philip should sleep in the attic so that he would not be frightened and alone, who had finally lost her temper on Jo's behalf, not her own, who had thought his mother might be consoled by a funny photograph, when he had forgotten even to wonder how she was getting along.

These thoughts were torture to Philip. In a moment of despair, he disliked himself even more than he thought other people must dislike him. But through the pain, far down within him, a new person began to grow.

He must have dozed with the light on, because, when the soft knock on the door aroused him, he had not been aware of any warning footsteps. He sat up wildly, thinking it must be Susan, but it was Jane, in her old-fashioned nightie and blue dressing gown, with her hair wet and curly from the bath. She was carrying a small tray with a glass of milk, and a plate containing two buns, fatly spread with butter and jam.

'I thought you might need a little extra supper,' she said, putting down the tray across his knees. 'There's nothing like a good rage for giving you an appetite.'

'How do you know?' asked Philip.

'Ah, well.' Jane sat down on the end of the bed, and looked at him pensively. 'It would be an unusual Gilmore who didn't have a temper. My memory hasn't totally deserted me. But passions cool with age. Eat your buns.'

Philip ate the buns and drank the milk, under her solemn but not unfriendly gaze. He was extraordinarily pleased that she had come. It was like when she had asked him to call her Jane, and when the supper was late because she was reading his *Beanos*. He felt that she had conferred some special honour upon him. Which was silly, of course, because most of the time she seemed not even to notice him, and he felt nothing for her that seemed to him like affection. She was too strange and remote for that. Even if she could find mistakes in a Professor's calculations, and cook like a dream, he still thought what he had always thought, that she was a funny old bird. Or that was what he thought he thought. Yet he was glad that she had come.

When he had finished, she took the tray away from him, and said gently, 'Philip. I can remember how bored I was, at your age, when I had to listen to unwanted advice from old people, and I swore I'd never do this when I was old myself. So forgive me—it's just that I hate to see you so unhappy. I know that things have happened which must have hurt you deeply, but please—if you're angry or upset, try not to take it out on other people. I know very well the temptation, but you only end up hurting them, and making yourself more miserable than when you started. And don't quarrel with Susan. She loves having you here, and she's a good girl.'

Then Philip knew that she had heard everything. And he was going to defend himself, to point out that it was Susan who had attacked him. But he managed not to.

'I know she is,' he said.

To his surprise, Jane waited until he lay down, and tucked his duvet closely around him, as if she had been tucking in children all her life. Then she switched off the light, and opened the door.

'Jane.'

He had to ask her. Perhaps, just perhaps, he had been wrong.

'Yes.'

'Jane, do you think I'm like your father?'

Her face was in the shadow now, but when she spoke, he could almost have sworn that she was laughing.

'I don't know you well enough to say. He was considered very good looking when he was young. Good night.'

He heard her go into the room next door, and the low murmur of her voice, and Susan's.

Philip felt deadly tired, as if he had just got into bed at the end of a long journey. Away at the back of his mind, something was niggling, something that he had noticed somewhere, and should remember, but couldn't. And he didn't care. Before the niggling could become a proper worry, he was asleep.

12

A Calmer Day

'White rabbits,' said Susan politely next morning, meeting Philip on the attic stair.

She believed—or said she did—that it was very unlucky to pass someone on the stairs, without uttering these magic words to cancel the misfortune.

Philip said, 'White rabbits,' on the grounds that in this house it was better to be safe than sorry, and clattered on down to the bathroom. He wondered, as he ran hot water into the bath from an incredibly old-fashioned gas geyser, whether Jane had also advised Susan to bury the hatchet. He decided that it was probably better to try to behave as if nothing had happened, and so he did.

When he reached the dining-room, he found Jane, in her dressing-gown, and Susan, dressed, already at the table. Susan had received a letter from her father in the morning post, and was relaying the news from Kenya to Jane, between mouthfuls of cornflakes.

'He's got a new Mercedes. And a dog. Its name's Chinga. Dobermann Pinscher. Oh, and Jane, he's got a new girl friend. Her name's Miranda Sturrock. She's a personal assistant. He says she's a lovely girl.'

' 'Twas ever thus,' murmured Jane, turning over a page of the *Herald*, and folding it so that she could prop it against the teapot.

'Oh, and listen,' Susan went on. 'He's probably being sent to Saudi Arabia in the spring, but before that he has to come to London, so he's going to fly up and spend a couple of nights with us. He says he'd like to see me, especially as it won't be convenient for me to spend the summer with him next year. Jane! Did you hear that? I don't have to go

74

to Saudi Arabia next summer. Gosh, that's great.'

'Don't you want to go to Saudi Arabia?' demanded Philip, shocked that anyone would so lightly dismiss an opportunity to visit that magical land of jet travel, private swimming pools, oil millionaires and burning sand. He would have loved to go. But Susan only laughed.

'I'd hate it,' she said frankly. 'It wouldn't be so bad if it was just him and me, but I'm scared of his dogs, and I never get on with his girl friends. Besides, I'd miss the Guide Camp, and me and Jane are maybe going to Tiree, aren't we, Jane?'

'So you keep telling me,' said Jane. She moved the newspaper to get at the teapot, and, as she poured herself another cup, continued, 'Now Philip—while I remember. Such a nice woman telephoned. Her name is Mrs Cawley, and she said she was a friend of yours. She wanted to know if you'd have lunch at her house today, and go to a football match with—Russell, is it?—and his father in the afternoon. Not at Ibrox, the other place. Celtic Park. I said I thought you almost certainly would want to, but that you'd ring her back, if not. She's going to send me her recipe for Redcurrant Fool. I think I have redcurrants somewhere, though I'd probably need a machete to reach them. Where does Mrs Cawley live, Philip?'

Philip refrained from pointing out that she'd had this information already.

'Maxie Court,' he told her again. 'It's one of these multi-storey blocks, just off the Scotland Road.'

'Oh, yes. I know where you mean,' said Jane. 'Now that's where I'd like to live. In a multi-storey block, right at the very top. No garden, no rooms upstairs, and a lovely view right across the river. I think I'll go to the City Chambers next time I'm in town, and put my name down on the list.'

'That will be the day,' said Susan cynically.

Philip was delighted at the prospect of lunch and football with the Cawleys, especially after last night's rumpus, and the strain of the last few days. Eagerly he got out his striped football hat and scarf, and cycled away

75

much muffled up, although the weather had turned warm again. As usual, he enjoyed the Scotch pies, and the telly, and the football, and the undemanding friendliness of the Cawleys. Mrs Cawley had written out the Redcurrant Fool recipe for Jane, and gave it to Philip, with instructions not to forget to give it to his auntie, who was so keen to have it. Philip was pleased that Jane and Mrs Cawley had liked each other—Mrs North and Mrs Cawley were not on such good terms—although just how they had got to the point of discussing recipes on a first phone call was mysterious. Unless you reckoned that Mrs Cawley's Glasgow friendliness would cut through the reserve of anyone who wasn't hopelessly prejudiced. He told Mrs Cawley what Jane had said about needing a machete to get at her redcurrants, intending to make her laugh, but Mrs Cawley was more appalled than amused.

'Aw, tell her she can mak' the Fool oot o' a tin, Philip,' she said. Then, shaking her head, 'That's fair terrible, though, is it no'? Puir body, she shouldna be livin' in hoose like that at her age. It'll juist get mair an' mair oan tap o'her. She'd be far better aff in ane o' thae wee pensioners' flats they've built oot at Sillerwood.'

'That's what she says,' Philip agreed, and watched Mrs Cawley being favourably impressed by old Miss Gilmore's common sense.

'She'll be ane o' thae bakery Gilmores?' Mrs Cawley enquired, and Philip had to nod, wondering why on earth he had bothered to keep his family background under his hat.

One thing spoiled his day. Or perhaps not exactly spoiled it, but acted all through it rather like an itchy midge bite, in a place where you couldn't get at it to scratch. It was in his mind, a feeling, which he had had since Jane switched out his light last night, that he had forgotten something. It was something which he had seen, or perhaps heard, with a flash of recognition, but which had flown at once from a mind too upset to hold onto it. The knowledge that this had happened flittered constantly on the edge of consciousness, but the image, if image it was, refused to return. It would not have mattered so much if he had not felt, anxiously, that it was something important. Even as he roared encouragement to his team, sang football songs, and drank Coke with Russ in the back of the car on the way home, the worry was there, nagging and itching and being a perfect pest.

When he got back to Wisteria Avenue, Susan asked him if he would like to watch *The Golden Years of Laurel and Hardy* on television after supper. He said he would, and they did, and went up to bed at ten o'clock.

It was midnight when Philip awoke, and remembered. Just like that. Instantly he slipped out of bed, and ran barefoot to Susan's room, switching on her light as he went in.

'Sue! Sue! Wake up!'

He pulled back her duvet, and shook her frantically into consciousness.

'What is it? Have we overslept? Is there a fire?'

Susan groped for the vanished duvet and sat up, looking like a terrified mouse with her astonished, sleepy eyes.

'No, but I've just remembered something very interesting,' Philip told her proudly.

Susan peered at the hands on her alarm clock, then narrrowed her eyes nastily at Philip.

'Hell's teeth,' she said in annoyance. 'Five past ruddy midnight, and you have just remembered something interesting. Couldn't it wait till morning? Do you realise that I lead a very busy life, and I need my beauty sleep, and—'

'Oh, don't go on,' interrupted Philip, bursting out laughing. 'You're so lovely already, and this *is* interesting. So just shut up, and listen.'

Susan flounced under the duvet again, but Philip knew that she was listening, all right. The duvet looked as if it had ears of its own. He sat down on the bean bag, and switched on the electric heater. 'I was trying to remember all day yesterday,' he went on, 'but I couldn't, till now. On

Friday night, when you were pitching in to me in the dining-room—'

'You're not going to bring that up again, I hope?' demanded Susan, poking her face accusingly out of the bed clothes.

'No! Now, please, will you shut up?' said Philip, and the face disappeared again. 'When you whirled me round, to make me look at Jane's old father, I saw something, only at the time I was too shook-up to pay attention. And afterwards I just couldn't remember—as I said, until now.' There was no reply, but the duvet continued to look alert, so he went on, 'You don't really notice, because the background's so dark, and you really only look at his face, don't you? But—you remember that desk in the photo-graph, Sue? The one I told you is in our sitting room at home? Well, it's in the portrait. He's standing behind it, but this is what might be important, as well as interesting. There's a box on the desk, a wooden one, with a pattern on it made out of darker wood—'

'Inlaid,' said Susan, who had emerged, and now was looking at him with all the attention he could desire.

'Very likely. Well the thing is, that box is in our house too. It's on the top shelf, in the cupboard on the landing. I can't remember anyone ever taking it down and opening it, but that's where it is.'

'And tomorrow is Sunday!' crowed Susan, in delight. 'We can go to your house after breakfast. Oh, Philip, you have been clever!'

78

13

A Letter for Hamish Gilmore

At ten o'clock next morning, Philip and Susan left Jane in the dining-room, doing the *Sunday Times* crossword puzzle, and set out on foot for Philip's house. The last fronds of an early morning mist were dispersing above the river, and the city lay quietly shining under a clear sky. The Park was beautiful with the last great gold and russet flaunting of the trees; in a few days it would be November, when they might any time be stripped in one remorseless night of wind and rain. There were few people, and little traffic about, and they got to Tarbet Gardens, the neat little street of modern houses where Philip lived, in less than twenty minutes. Susan waited at the gate of number four while Philip went to fetch the key; when he came back they went up the short path, and Philip opened the front door.

There was a flurry of letters and circulars on the mat inside; Philip gathered them up, and put them on the table in the hall. The house had the enclosed, slightly unpleasant smell of a place temporarily abandoned, a mixture of the last meal eaten, the withered flowers which no one had remembered to throw away, and the disinfectant put down the lavatory. Philip, who was hating every second of this, went noisily into the kitchen and opened the back door, saying a bit too heartily, 'Poo! What a niff! I'd better give the place an airing while I'm here.'

When he came back, Susan had gone into the tiny dining-room, and was looking around her in delight.

'Oh, Philip!' she exclaimed longingly. 'What a lovely house! If only Jane and I could have a house like this!' Philip watched her skipping from the dining-room to the sitting-room, then into the kitchen, remarking on the convenience of little boxy rooms, fitted carpets, double glazing and ceilings which you could paint standing on a stool. She ran to the back door, and stood looking out into the tiny, square garden, with its woven fencing, two small cherry trees and three trim flowerbeds.

'Lovely,' she said. 'Jane could sit in a garden chair on this nice little patio, and I could cut the grass. No horrible groves of bamboo. It's absolutely super.'

It was not what Philip thought. He knew that this was the most ordinary of houses, the kind of place everyone lived in who aspired to more than a Council flat, and less than a posh conversion in Wisteria Avenue. It was all right, but you lived in it without ever really noticing it. He let Susan go exploring upstairs on her own, and when she came down, recalled her attention to the matter in hand.

'What shall we look at first—box or desk?' he asked.

'Desk,' said Susan, and they went into the sitting-room, with its tweedy chairs, and Mr North's unseen presence on the sofa. The desk stood under the window, a dark, handsome piece of furniture, with some china ladies and a bowl of withered dahlias on top.

'There's nothing worth looking at in the drawers,' Philip told Susan, 'so you needn't be embarrassed. Some of them have sewing patterns and gardening catalogues in them, that's all.'

'Which one doesn't open?' Susan enquired.

'The top one, on the right. Why don't we take out all the drawers that will come out, and feel around at the back, just in case anything has dropped down?'

'Good thinking,' approved Susan. She helped Philip to pull out all the deep, narrow drawers, then they squatted down, and felt about with their fingers inside the inner casing of the desk. But, as Philip had predicted, in vain. 'I wish we could think of a way of opening the locked drawer,' Susan sighed wistfully, as Philip slotted the loose ones back into place.

'Well, we just can't,' said Philip, definitely. 'It's been tried before, believe me, and it won't unlock. And if we tried to force it, there would be hell to pay when Mum got back—for me, remember, not for you. So forget it. Now, let's go upstairs and look at the box.'

Susan followed him, and when Philip had fetched out a little aluminium step-ladder, he lifted down from the cupboard shelf the dusty, walnut inlaid box which old William Gilmore had kept on his desk, half a century ago. It opened without difficulty, and Philip spilled the contents out on the brown carpet of the landing. He and Susan stared at them, as their optimism melted away.

At first, it really did seem that once again a good idea had come to nothing. Long ago, the box apparently had been used to hold pens, pencils, paper-clips, sealing wax—the usual desk clutter of a man of business fifty years before. Then, as often happens, rubbish had found its way in as well—rusty pen-nibs, pencil shavings, crumpled invoices, a broken penknife. There were two letters, in envelopes bearing stamps with the head of a bearded king, but when Philip took out the enclosures, they saw that they were business letters from strangers, and of no interest at all. The only other things in the box were a dirty white envelope without a direction, and half a sheet of letter paper, torn through the middle and crushed carelessly into a loose ball. Philip turned back the flap of the envelope, and shook out what at first looked like two small squares of thin card. But when they turned them over, the children saw that they were really photographs. Alerted suddenly, they hurried with them to the landing window, and laid them on the sill.

They were old-fashioned black and white snapshots, printed on shiny paper; Susan and Philip looked at them with an interest which was not pleasurable. The first one showed a much younger, but not young, Jane, sitting on the front doorstep at *The Mount*, with a cat curled up on her lap. She was wearing a dark frock, which had probably been as unfashionable then as those she wore now; her dense black hair drifted around a face which had the oddly unfinished look which young faces have in photographs, if we have only known them old. Not surprisingly, she had declined to smile for the camera, and her dark, thoughtful, reticent eyes were the most familiar thing about her.

The second photograph had been taken indoors, and it made Susan feel cold and sick inside. It showed a very old man, so shrunken that he seemed almost to be held together by his plaid dressing-gown, asleep in an arm-chair. He had a rug over his knees and a cushion under his almost hairless head, which fell sideways, open-mouthed and most unpleasant to look at. He was no more than the dried husk of the man in the portrait, whose great grandchildren were afraid to face him over the supper table.

'Your Dad's handiwork, I suppose,' said Philip.

'Yes. He really was a little beast,' said Susan distaste-fully. 'You shouldn't take photographs of people like that. It's indecent.'

Philip could not help agreeing. He put the photograph back in the envelope, and put it in his jerkin pocket. With feelings of depression and anti-climax, he began to pick up the ancient junk on the carpet, and toss it back into the box. Susan, meanwhile, badly shaken by the photographs, idly picked up the small, crumpled ball of writing paper, and smoothed it out on the window sill. She was scarcely aware of what she was doing, and she had read the first few lines of writing before it dawned on her what this actually was.

Then, 'Philip!' she cried.

The note in her voice, half way between a sob and a cry of triumph, lifted Philip in one leap across the landing. Susan pointed with a trembling finger, and he read the words written on the scruffy paper in a firm, copperplate hand.

London,
3 April 1940

My dear Hamish,
　　We move out tonight, and I write in haste to
beg you to give the enclosed to Jane. I dare not risk

sending it direct—I am certain your father has
intercepted my letters before now, and I shall take no
chances with this one, on which all my future happiness
depends. God knows how this is to end. Your father's
prejudice against me, as an employee of the firm, and as
a gardener's son, seems entrenched beyond change. But
you, I know, will continue to take my part, and my
Jane—

But what of his Jane they would never know, for the
paper had been ripped away under her name, and the back
was blank. The children stared at each other, Philip
blowing out his pink cheeks in astonishment, Susan's eyes
filling with tears. When she had recovered a little, she said
in a tight, angry voice, 'So it was Hamish Gilmore who
was to blame. He was the one who got the letter, and the
ring—that must have been what 'the enclosed' meant, and
no one else would have opened a letter addressed to him,
would they? But he didn't give it to Jane. Oh, why not,
Philip? He was Ewan MacNeill's best friend   it said so in
the press cutting we found—and he was Jane's favourite
brother. Oh, why didn't he help them?'
Philip could not think of any answer, and hopelessly
shook his head.
Susan folded up the paper, smoothing out its wrinkled
surface with unsteady fingers.
'Do you suppose it would be stealing, if I took this home
with me?' she asked wistfully. 'I'd rather like to keep it, if
you think it's OK.'
'Of course it's OK,' Philip assured her. 'Would you like
Jane's photograph too?'
But Susan said no, she didn't think she wanted that.
Philip left her to have a little cry while he locked up, and
went to the garden shed to fetch his father's tool bag; when
he had returned the key to Mrs Balloch, they set off again
across the Park.
'What are you going to do with that?' asked Susan,
looking at the canvas bag.

'Mend that stupid gate,' said Philip, 'before Jane goes head first into the undergrowth.'

'That's nice of you,' Susan said.

The Park was full of people now, flying kites, playing ball games, swooping about on bicycles. But Susan and Philip walked apart from each other, each occupied with very private thoughts.

Susan was thinking of Ewan MacNeill, robbed of his life more than thirty years before she was born. He had written to his girl and sent the ring, feeling safe to entrust his future happiness to his friend; he had gone to his death unaware, at least, that that friend had betrayed him, and Jane been doomed to spend her life believing that she was the one who had been betrayed. Pity for the aloof, gentle, distrustful Jane she knew mingled in Susan with a passion of rage against Hamish Gilmore, who had taken the part of a friend, and had acted the part of an enemy. It was not his fault that Ewan MacNeill had died, but it was his fault that his sister had suffered so unfairly, and so very long.

Philip's thoughts were of a different kind. One phrase in the letter had shocked him so deeply that, for the moment, he could hardly think of anything else. Ewan MacNeill had been a gardener's son. The address in the newspaper had obscured this fact; Mr and Mrs Albert MacNeill were not the owners of *Winterwood*, but servants there, he the gardener and she—the housekeeper, perhaps. It didn't matter. It was the similarity to his mother's situation which confounded Philip. Proud old William Gilmore had not wanted his only daughter to marry a gardener's son. Thirty years later, he had not wanted his grand-daughter to marry a shipyard labourer's son, the young man from the Bank who had become Philip's father. And there in the Park, as he trudged solitary by the side of the boating pond, shuffling in leaves, Philip realised the truth about Jane. It might be true, as Susan had said, that she could have taken a brilliant degree at University, and done something distinguished with her life. But that would have been second best to her. What she wanted was to marry a young man who worked as a clerk in her father's business, and—because Ewan MacNeill could never have earned a lot of money, and her father would have given her none—to have lived with him in a little house with a mortgage, and an insurance policy with the Sun Life Assurance Company, in case anything went wrong. And perhaps Ewan MacNeill would have bawled at his kid, and turned off the telly, and worn a soppy kilt on Sundays, and been bald by the time he was thirty seven. But Jane wouldn't have minded, any more than her niece had minded . . . he had never allowed himself to think of it before, but now, when he remembered the terrible, stifled sobbing of his mother, alone in her bed at night since his father had died, Philip understood what the loss of Ewan MacNeill had meant to Jane. And he grieved for her, and he grieved for his mother, and it was the first time in his life that he had ever grieved for anyone other than himself.

But why, oh why, thought Philip, had his parents not realised that Jane, of all people, would understand their predicament, and sympathise? Surely it must have been obvious that she was the last person in the world to mind that his father had not been educated at Glasgow Academy, and was a teller in the Clydesdale Bank at Bishopbriggs? Yet they had always said that she was hard and proud, and had made bitter and unkind remarks about her which Philip now knew were untrue. They had made a stranger of her when she needed them as friends, and had hurt her, Philip suspected, more than they had ever known.

The explanation came to him as he crossed the railway bridge, and began to trudge up Cliff Road, the only possible explanation, he was sure. His mother could never have known that once, thirty years before, her aunt had been in the same position as herself. What was it Susan had said? That it was her father who had told her Jane's story, because Jane never would. Jane had closed her lips over the sad tale of the past, and had taken all the consequences, because she could not, or would not tell.

14

Visions Rising

Lunch that day was a totally silent meal. Jane, never exactly talkative, frequently read at the table, and did so now, glad perhaps to be free from perpetual interruptions beginning, 'Jane, listen,' or, 'Hey, Jane, did you know . . . ' Or perhaps she simply didn't notice. Had she looked closely at the flushed, sober faces of her companions, she might have seen that something was amiss. Had she known that, since breakfast time, she had become a wronged and tragic heroine in their eyes, it is hard to say whether she would have been more surprised, or annoyed.

After the meal was over, Susan went off upstairs to do her homework, and Philip, after he had struggled to take the gate off its hinges, and staggered with it up the tunnel to the vestibule at the front door, set to work to saw and plane five centimetres off its bottom edge. He was glad to have something that he could do for Jane, for he was angry and miserable on her behalf. In the Park that morning, his defences had finally gone down, and he found that he cared, more than he could have believed possible, for an injustice inflicted on someone else. And, because it was his first experience of this feeling, he was only now discovering how that caring hurts more than the pain of an injustice inflicted upon oneself. Later, he would write to his mother, and tell her that there was a wrong to be put right, but first he would mend the gate for Jane.

She came out of the house while he was working, and stood watching him, with an expression of cautious gratitude on her face.

'It's very good of you, Philip,' she said, 'but you will be careful not to cut off any fingers, won't you? Your mother

86

wouldn't be pleased, and I'd be sure to get the blame.'

Philip sat back on his heels, wiped the sweat from his forehead, and gave her the wide grin which would have brought a smiling response from anyone else in the world.

'They sew fingers back on now,' he told her. 'I expect all you need is a needle and thread. You're a scientist—you could probably do it for me.'

Dammit, he thought. One day he would make her smile. But not today, apparently.

'I'm not a scientist,' she said, 'and I don't think I'd be very good at sewing on fingers. I can't see well enough to thread a needle. So please—do be careful.'

She shivered slightly, drawing her cardigan more closely around her, and was about to go back indoors when, on a sudden impulse, Philip said, 'Jane. Please, I want to ask you something.'

'Yes. What is it?'

She stopped, and turned, propping herself against the side post of the inner door.

'Jane, when my Mum was young—did you know her very well?'

It was one of the good things about her that she never asked you why you wanted to know things. She either answered you, or not, as she saw fit. Now, she said, 'No, I didn't, Philip. I knew Alex, Susan's father, better, I suppose. By the time your mother was growing up, my father was very old, and needed a great deal of my attention, and then—wasn't she away at boarding school for a while? I hardly remember. Anyway, although we lived for a long time in the same house, Margaret and I, we certainly had very little opportunity to get to know each other.'

This was what Philip had suspected, and it explained a lot. But now, encouraged perhaps by her easy response, he blurted out a less prudent question.

'Jane, is it true that the Gilmores didn't want my Mum to marry my Dad?'

She had been turning away again, but now she turned sharply back, and Philip saw for the first time in her a flash of the famous Gilmore temper. Perhaps some passions did not cool with age. Her brown eyes hardened, a faint flush rose on her pallid cheeks, and she said irascibly, 'I have absolutely no idea. I lived in this house for nearly sixty years with Gilmores, and I doubt that I ever knew what any of them thought about anything. If you mean me, I assure you, the only thought I ever had on the subject was, "Good luck to them."'

With which she left him, abruptly.

Philip took the annoyance of adults in his stride; it was what he was used to, and he certainly preferred that Jane should look at him crossly, than that she should not look at him at all. But today, particularly, he did not want to offend her, so, when he had finished mending the gate, he decided that he would go into the dining-room, and apologise. It was a pretty cheeky question, after all, but it had just slipped out. When he went into the hall, however, Jane had come to the dining-room door, and, before he could open his mouth, was apologising to him.

'Philip, please forgive me. I oughtn't to have snapped at you. It was just so unexpected—it had never occurred to me that children of yet another generation might be troubled by these sad old tales of misunderstanding. And what you must have been thinking of me all these weeks, I hate to imagine. However—the answer to your question is that I don't think the Gilmores minded who Margaret married as much as they minded—that is, I mean, would have minded—thirty years earlier. They had become less grand with the passing of time. If you don't mind my saying so, perhaps your parents imagined that they—or we—minded more than was the case.'

Philip didn't mind her saying so; it was exactly what he had come to believe himself.

When Philip went back upstairs, Susan was still busy with her homework, and he knew better by now than to interrupt her. So, while he was waiting for her to finish, he got out his painting of the drawing-room downstairs, which he had never found time to complete, and spread it out on the bed to look at it. He thought that it was really quite good. He was a better-than-average artist for his age, with a fine sense of perspective, and his drawing of the long, high room, folding in towards the peaked, church-like windows at the end, was effective. His colour work, he knew, was less perfect, but since it was all done by guessing, perhaps it didn't matter too much. He fetched a pencil, and did a little more decorative work on the frame around the looking-glass above the fireplace. But the lack of pictures spoiled the composition; all these expanses of washed brown wall were quite wrong.

Philip was considering this problem when Susan came in.

'I've done nearly everything,' she announced. 'Luckily, I had less than usual today. I'll ask Jane to help me with the Maths after supper, because I really don't know where to begin. What are you doing Philip?'

Philip explained about the pictures.

'I do agree about not taking any more photographs,' he said, 'especially after finding that horrid one of the old man this morning. Imagine how awful it would be if he turned up in one we had taken! And anyway, even if I did know what the pictures in the drawing-room looked like, I couldn't show them properly on such a small scale. But I was thinking—if we took my painting down to the empty room, and laid it on the floor, I could see where there are maps on the walls, and put them in the right position on the painting. Then I'd just paint in blobs and squiggles, and frames, later on.'

'Mn,' said Susan. 'Yes. Well, I suppose so.'

Philip could sense her reluctance, and understood it. He too felt, sometimes, that they were meddling with things which were abnormal, and which might erupt into an experience very alarming indeed. Yet some force which he didn't understand compelled him to go on. It was not that he felt very brave, or merely curious; he was convinced that it was important, and that all the information they had amassed was leading to some discovery—only, as yet, he did not know what. And he thought that, whether she admitted it or not, Susan really felt the same. Now she glanced at her watch, and at the grey rectangle of Philip's sky light.

'Well, all right,' she agreed, 'but we mustn't be long. Now that the hour has changed, it'll be dark early, and I just don't fancy being down there when night falls.'

'This will only take ten minutes,' said Philip reassuringly.

It was ten past four when they pushed open the door of the empty drawing-room, and slipped inside. Out of doors, the mist which had swathed the Clyde valley in the morning was returning as the sun went down. Beyond the windows, the decaying garden hung motionless as if behind grey net, and the sun was a silver-rose circle, on a denser curtain to the west. The light in the room was sufficient to see by, but less than they had expected.

They could never agree, afterwards, when exactly they had noticed that something was different. Susan said, not until they had been in for some little time, but Philip thought that, as he went in, he sensed that the room was not, as it should have been, entirely empty. He certainly remembered something which had occurred to him weeks ago, after he had been in this room for the first time. It did not feel as it appeared. It felt like a room from which people had gone out, only a few minutes before. And Philip noticed now, as he and Susan walked uncertainly over the bare floorboards, that it was not cool and airy, as an empty room ought to be. It felt—absurd as it might seem—like the sitting-room which Jane called Gilmore's Repository, stuffy, overcrowded, warm. Perhaps all of this dawned upon Susan more slowly, and that was why she said suddenly, with great urgency, 'Come on. Let's get your job done, and get out of here. It's beginning to get dark.'

'Right,' Philip agreed.

He unrolled his picture in the middle of the floor, and Susan knelt to hold down the sides for him, as it tended to curl itself up again. He took a pencil out of his pocket, scrutinised the walls, and transferred the outlines of the dark patches to the buff-coloured walls of his painting. There were three quite large ones, two smaller ones, between the bookcase and the chest of drawers, and two groups, each of three tiny ones, on either side of the window. The biggest of all, about three metres by two metres, was above the place where old William Gilmore's desk had once stood.

'I wonder what that one was?' Philip said, more to break the oppressive silence than to draw an answer from the taut, unhappy Susan. And even as he spoke, something terrible happened—for the answer was not spoken, but revealed. The great dark shadow on the wall suddenly whitened, and then, like a photograph in a bowl of developer, the picture formed itself unhurriedly before the children's frightened eyes. Susan had never seen that picture before, and never would, because for years it had been in a private collection in America, but she would remember every detail of it until the day she died. And Philip, as he gazed, understood at last why Jane Gilmore had found it so difficult to look him in the face.

In a heavy, gilded frame, three bronze-headed boys and a dark-eyed girl stared out solemnly through branches ornate with leaves, and a scattering of stiff white flowers. Boys in tweed jackets and high collars, the girl in blue, with a ribboned braid of thick black hair lying over her shoulder. And she was Jane, and she was Susan, and the boys were William, and Thomas, and Hamish, but they were also Philip, all of them were Philip, at twelve, and ten, and seven. And, afraid as they were, Susan and Philip could have gazed and gazed, and gone on gazing.

But now they noticed that, as the light faded, the rest of the room was developing itself too. Tables and chairs, bookcase and chest of drawers gradually took to themselves a substance which was not tangible, yet was, to the eye, real. For perhaps twenty seconds, Susan and Philip looked wildly around, their power to think and move suspended, then Philip recovered his. Snatching up his painting from the carpet which had formed like thin flesh on the bones of the floor, he grabbed Susan's hand and hauled her after him to the door. He wrenched it open, and they tumbled out together onto the landing, their breath coming in vast sobs.

'Oh, Philip,' moaned Susan. 'Oh, Philip! Oh, Jane!'

It was the most terrifying thing that had ever happened to either of them in their lives; Susan said, more terrifying than her encounter with a snake in Kenya, Philip said more terrifying than thinking there was a burglar in the next room. In the short term, it was the need to appear normal in front of Jane, at supper time, which enabled the children to pull themselves together; the last thing they wanted was to have Jane becoming suspicious that something odd was going on. In the longer term, they were steadied by their determination, often repeated during the next few days, that they would never, never enter that empty room—so miscalled—again. And, had there been the slightest wavering in their resolution, something which they saw a few nights later would certainly have hardened it once more.

On the Wednesday of the following week, there was a Parents' Evening at Susan's school, to which Jane had said she would go, so that she could report to her nephew on Susan's progress. Jane took matters of education very seriously, and felt that it was time to take advice about the subjects which Susan should study next year. When, on Tuesday evening after supper, Susan announced that she and Philip intended to accompany her, to make sure that she was not mugged and robbed in the West End, her response was at first incredulous, then exasperated.

'I have never heard anything so ridiculous in my life,' she said. 'For heaven's sake, child, have you ever looked at me? Do you suppose any criminal in his right mind would think that I had a thousand pounds concealed in my corsets?'

Susan could not help laughing inordinately at this, but Philip said sternly, 'Listen, Jane. You just don't understand. People aren't mugged for a thousand pounds, they're mugged for sixty pence. Anyway, you should be grateful that you have two tough bodyguards like us, ready to look after you. You're far too independent. Honestly, I don't know what old ladies are coming to.'

And perhaps she was grateful, for she changed her mind, and said not only that they could come, but that she would give herself a night off cooking, and take them out to supper afterwards—which she did. After Jane had done her duty at the school, they went to an Italian restaurant in Great Western Road, where the children ate hugely, and Jane sparsely, just as at home. Susan and Philip, who were out in the evening as seldom as Jane, enjoyed themselves exuberantly, and perhaps she enjoyed herself too, watching them. Her memory stirred by her visit to her old school, she told them, in her dry, unsmiling fashion, some hilarious stories about things that had happened there fifty years ago, leading Susan to remark severely that there must have been more hooligans and vandals in Glasgow in the Thirties than in the Eighties. Jane agreed with this, and said that a large number of them had lived in Wisteria Avenue.

But when they came out of the restaurant, the weather had turned damp and icy; they had to wait for a long time for a bus, and Philip and Susan could see Jane becoming cold and miserable and exhausted. She seemed to go away from them then, into the private world she inhabited; in the bus she sat huddled in her coat, with her collar turned up, staring out into the night city with dark, tired eyes. She would have sat on past their stop, if Susan had not touched her lightly on the arm, and said, 'Jane dear, we're nearly home.' So she followed them, and walked silently between them up Knightshill Road, no doubt longing for her bed. And both Philip and Susan would gladly have offered her an arm to lean on, but did not, for fear of being rebuffed. Short-sighted and never very observant, however, she fortunately did not see what the children saw, as they turned the corner into Wisteria Avenue. There was no moon, and no street light, despite the attempts of the

Residents' Association to acquire one. The Gothic sil-houette of *The Mount,* rising out of it ruff of shrubs, appeared only as a mass of black on very dark grey. Which was why the children's young eyes, neither short-sighted nor unobservant, were immediately drawn upwards to the light which ought not to have been there. A thin, vertical slice of brightness, it shone out between curtains not completely closed across the windows of a room that was untenanted, and where the curtains were never drawn.

After Jane had locked the door, she said, 'Thank you for looking after me. Good night,' and went away thankfully to her room, leaving the children to climb the long, dark stair together. Philip had nothing to say; Susan spoke twice. As they passed the door of the room where the eerie light shone, she said, 'Only people can draw curtains, Philip.' And on the attic landing, before she went into her bedroom, she said, 'Never again. Never. Never in a thousand years.'

Perhaps it was because he too was convinced that he would never, in a thousand years, dare to enter that room again, that Philip did what he did before he went to bed. Once more, he acted on a strange impulse, but this time in the belief that, for himself and Susan, he was putting the finishing touches to something which would not again concern them. Bringing out his uncle's black and white photographs from the chest of drawers, he found a pencil, and unrolled his painting of the room downstairs. First, he drew his great grandfather, in a chair by the fire. Only he made him look younger, dressing him in a suit like the one he wore in his portrait, and giving him more hair. And then he drew Jane, sitting on the fender in front of the fire, with her cat in her lap.

15

Accident

Now it was November. Fireworks had their season, wet yellow leaves lay like skin on the pavements of Knightshill, and glistening black trees were everywhere adrip. Each afternoon, fawnish fog slipped up the river, blanketing the low-lying parts of the city, and coiling lazily upwards into Wisteria Avenue. The old Gothic mansions took on the appearance of castles in a ghost story, with their pointed roofs and ornamental turrets wrapped in gauzy scarves of mist. In the garden of *The Mount,* every tree wept sadly, and Jane took to filling hot-water bottles for the children before she went off to bed.

For Philip and Susan, it was a waiting time. Although the light under the door continued to shine, they had no inclination to investigate further. The information in Ewan MacNeill's letter to Hamish Gilmore, interesting though it was, did not immediately seem to lead to any further discovery. So, as Susan said, there was nothing for it but to wait, and see what happened next. But what did happen was so unexpected, and so upsetting, that it drove all thoughts of eerie rooms and past events from their minds, for a considerable time to come.

On the eighth of November, which was a Tuesday, Philip went home with Russ after school. They had a snack and watched a video film, and it was after five when Philip cycled back through the Park, crossed over the main road at the railway bridge, and changed gear for the final sharp incline up Cliff Road and into Wisteria Avenue. Tuesday, Philip thought contentedly. Jane usually made a ham and egg pie on Tuesday. She might be a funny old bird, and she might not have a clue what was going on upstairs in her own house, but she was a damn good cook. Philip was going to miss her suppers, and her packed lunches, when his mother came home in a few weeks time. He could not have said at which precise moment it occurred to him that something was wrong, but, even before he got to the monkey puzzle, some extra sense alerted him to the fact that things were not just as they usually were.

There was a yellow Volvo estate car drawn up at the pavement outside *The Mount,* and that was unusual, for a start. When, forgetting his own handiwork, he bumped vigorously against the gate, and himself nearly fell into the rhododendrons, he recovered to notice that the front door was wide open, and that the only light switched on at the front of the house was in the hall. Normally, at this time, the light was on in the dining-room, as Jane moved in and out of the kitchen, laying the table for supper. So, even before he saw Susan, he had a faint warning that something out of the ordinary had occurred. But nothing could really have prepared him for what it was.

Susan was sitting on a chair in the dimly lit hall, and as soon as he saw her white, strained face, he knew that this was serious. She had not cried before she saw him, but when she did tears came into her eyes, and she ran to him, sobbing, 'Oh, Philip, thank God you've come! The most ghastly thing has happened. Jane has had an accident. She was run down by a motor-cycle at the traffic lights. Oh, Philip!'

Philip felt as if a damp hand stroked his face, making it chill. He stared fixedly at Susan in the thin electric light, while something hard tightened painfully around his chest. And in this dreadful moment, he acknowledged fully for the first time that Jane Gilmore was more to him that a funny old bird.

'It didn't—she's not—' His numb lips managed to form these words, but no more would come.

Susan shook her head vigorously. Perhaps Philip's obvious distress steadied her temporarily, for she managed to tell him, quite coherently, what had happened.

'Jane had to go in to town to the dentist,' she said. 'She

came back on the bus about two o'clock, and when she got off at the corner of Wishaw Street—oh, I don't know exactly how it happened, but when she was crossing the road at the traffic lights, a motor-cycle came out from behind the bus, and knocked her down. Mrs Forbes thinks that maybe Jane didn't see that the lights had changed.'

'Mrs Who?' enquired Philip. He could not recollect ever having heard this name before.

'Mrs Forbes. She lives at number ten. She was on the bus too, and got off when Jane did. She knew who Jane was, and she went with her in the ambulance to the Infirmary. She's been very kind, and promised Jane that she'd look after us. She's in Jane's room now, getting some things that she will need.'

It was all too much for poor Susan, who started to cry in real earnest, saying, 'Damn, damn,' and groping for her handkerchief.

Philip gave her his. It was reasonably clean, and better than nothing. Then he put down his schoolbag, which he was still clutching, and went across the hall towards Jane's bedroom. He met Mrs Forbes coming out. She was a fair, youngish woman in a sheepskin jacket; Philip had seen her before, walking her dogs on a Sunday morning. He said brusquely, 'I'm Philip. Thank you for helping us. Is Jane very badly hurt?'

He thought it would be better to know. But when Mrs Forbes had put down a small pile of clothing and a sponge bag on the hall chest, she said frankly, 'I'm afraid I can't tell you that, Philip. They took her straight into the Casualty Department at the Royal, and I came home. I would gladly have waited, but she was much more distressed by the thought of you two being alone than by the thought of being alone herself. I think her arm is probably broken, and there's some injury to her head— but she didn't lose consciousness, and she was talking perfectly sensibly. That's a very good sign. Now, look,' she went on robustly, 'crying isn't going to help, and if you don't stop now, Susan, Miss Gilmore will be very upset when I take you to see her in the evening. She has been very

97

brave, and you must be, too. Now please—go upstairs, and fetch your pyjamas and your toothbrushes. I can manage everything else. And please, bring me a carrier bag for Miss Gilmore's bits and pieces. Then we'll lock up here, and go round to my house. You'll feel better after you've had something to eat.'

For Susan, it was good advice. Whatever happened, she would not do anything which might upset Jane. She took a deep breath, dried her eyes, and went upstairs with Philip. Without a word, but glad of each other's company, they put the things they would need into the smaller of Philip's suitcases. Then they found a plastic carrier bag, and took it down to Mrs Forbes.

'That's fine,' she said. 'Now, come on. I've got the key, so if you'll put the hall light out, Philip, we'll be off.'

Mrs Forbes lived in the upstairs part of number ten, and at any other time Susan and Philip would have been fascinated to see what could be done to make a place like Jane's first floor into a modern, comfortable home. But now, they could not concentrate, and all they had was a floating impression of white walls, futuristic lighting, jungly plants and black furniture standing on a carpet as deep and green as a meadow. Mrs Forbes made them sit down on a squashy, comfortable sofa, and switched on a large white television set. Children's programmes were showing, and they stared blankly at the busy screen. Later, she brought them a picnic meal of fish fingers, baked beans and chips. At half-past six, after writing a note of explanation for her husband, she told them to put on their coats again, and took them out to the car.

The journey through the winter evening streets, the neon confusion of the hospital reception area, the long, long walk along draughty, hot, sweet-smelling corridors—it was the replay of a nightmare already experienced for Philip, whose father had been rushed to hospital three times before he died. It was another hospital, but it might have been the same. For Susan it was terrible, and new. She walked tight-mouthed, in a daze of disbelief, carrying Jane's belongings in the carrier bag. But she always

98

remembered afterwards that Philip, no doubt at some cost to his self-esteem, held her firmly by the elbow, and whispered from time to time, 'Don't worry. It's going to be all right.' They came at last to glass-paned doors, and after Mrs Forbes had spoken briefly to the nurse on duty in the little office outside, Philip and Susan were escorted by the nurse into a long, cream-walled ward.

Jane was in bed on the left, about halfway down. Her eyes were closed as they approached, and like all elderly people, she looked smaller lying down than she did when she was up and dressed. Her right arm and hand were bandaged, and supported on a pillow at her side; she had a large patch of sticking plaster on her forehead, and around her left cheekbone there was a mass of purple bruising, which seemed to run sideways, and disappear into her hair.

'Only ten minutes,' said the nurse firmly, as she drew blue striped curtains around the bed, making a roofless tent. 'She's very tired. I'll come back when time's up.'

Jane opened puzzled eyes when she heard the nurse's voice, but then she saw Susan, and held out her free hand to her. Susan ran to the bed, and grasped the offered hand convulsively; she was not crying, but, now that the time had come, all she could say, in a high, sobbing voice, was, 'Oh, Jane. Oh darling Jane!'

Then Philip, who was standing back, saw Jane focus her tired eyes on Susan, and the most extraordinary expression pass over her pale, damaged face. It was as if, in a flash of understanding, she accepted the truth of something she would never have dared even to hope for, and she looked at Susan as if she were seeing her for the very first time.

'My dear child,' she said weakly. 'Don't look like that. Susan, please, don't. I'm perfectly all right—not even any bones broken. A sprained arm, and some cuts and bruises, that's all. They'll send me home tomorrow. They've said so.'

Susan relaxed, just a little. She kept hold of Jane's hand, lifted it gently, and rubbed it against her cheek.

'I'll look after you,' she promised.

'Yes, I'm sure you will.' Jane closed her eyes again, and was silent for a moment. Then she made a great effort, and said, 'Susan, listen. Are you and Philip all right for tonight? That Mrs Forbes said she would look after you.'

'Yes, of course. She already has,' replied Susan, soothingly. 'We had tea at her house, and we're going to stay there overnight, so you mustn't worry about us at all. She brought us, and she's outside waiting for us now.'

Jane seemed relieved.

'Good,' she said. 'She seems such a nice, kind woman— but do you know, I don't remember that I ever saw her before.'

Philip decided that it was time for him to enter this conversation.

'You'd see your neighbours better, if you got your tropical rain forest cut down,' he remarked saucily. 'I'd do it myself, but my saw isn't big enough.'

Jane's sleepy eyes moved slowly from Susan to him, and she gave him her usual, gravely considering look.

'Hello, Impudence,' she said. 'How are you?'

'A lot better than when I thought you were dead,' admitted Philip.

'Oh, I see. Sorry,' Jane said.

'But I'll tell you what,' said Philip suddenly between his teeth, his face reddening as fury gripped him. 'If I just got my hands on that ruddy biker, I'd smash his stupid face in.'

Jane shook her head, winced, and closed her eyes again.

'So violent,' she murmured reprovingly. 'You Gilmore boys, you're all the same. He's been to see me. Poor young man, what a dreadful state he was in. A child in black leather. I had such trouble convincing him that it wasn't his fault.'

Philip, who had experience of hospital visiting, could see how exhausted she was, and struggling to keep awake against the drugs she had been given.

'Sorry,' he said. 'I just happen to like you, Jane.'

'Oh, dear. I can't imagine why. Susan—'

'Yes, Jane.'

'On the table. There's a brown envelope. Do you see it?'

'Yes, I do.'

'Will you take it, please, and keep it for me until I get home? It's a silly thing, really—no value—but I'd hate more than anything to lose it.'

Susan picked up the envelope, and put it away carefully in the zipped pocket inside her blazer.

'I'll keep it safe for you,' she said reassuringly.

At this point, the nurse returned, and told them it was time to go. Briskly she whisked the curtains back, destroying intimacy with a flick of her wrist. Susan leaned over Jane and kissed her, something Philip was certain she had never dared to do before, and obediently followed the nurse. Philip went after them a few paces, then suddenly stopped, and darted back to Jane's bedside.

'Hey, Jane,' he hissed, close to the pillow. 'Just you wait till you see yourself in a mirror! You'll have a fit! I'm telling you—you're going to have the most fantastic keeker you ever saw in your life—like you'd gone twelve rounds in the ring at the Kelvin Hall!'

There was a pause. And then, in this most unlikely situation, Philip won his battle. Jane did not open her eyes, but as he watched her, the corners of her mouth turned slowly upwards, and she laughed. And it was not a harsh, elderly cackle, but a round, clear hoot of young laughter, as if she had been keeping it in store from her girlhood, and was giving it to Philip now.

Susan had not meant to take Jane's treasure out of the brown envelope with 'Greater Glasgow Health Board' printed on it. But the flap had not been sealed, and at bed time, when she and Philip were together in the huge 'studio bedroom' which had been made out of all the servants' rooms at number ten, she found that the contents had fallen out into her blazer pocket.

'Look, Philip,' she said, drawing out a long gold chain, to which was looped an oval of gold framing a small, black and white photograph. She held it up to the light, and examined it wonderingly. 'I've never seen her wear this,' she went on. 'It's a bit of a locket, I think. Yes—look—here's where the other half should be joined on. She must have lost it. What a shame.'

With his heart beating faster than usual, Philip came over in his striped pyjamas to the camp bed where Susan was going to sleep.

'Let me see,' he said, careful not to sound excited.

Susan held out her hand, and on the palm Philip saw the familiar gold oval, but this time enclosing an undamaged photograph, showing the head and shoulders of a merry young man in a white shirt.

'Ewan, I suppose,' Susan said sadly.

'Yes, I suppose so,' Philip agreed. 'Poor old Jane.'

He didn't want to talk any more, so he went and got into his bed on the other side of the room, pulling the covers over his head. He felt very tired; like all awful days, this one had seemed endless, even if the awfulness had only begun at five o'clock. He also felt a little mean, because he hadn't shared with Susan what she would certainly have shared with him, but even now, he wasn't going to tell her. Jane would be the first to know. And, as he drifted away into sleep, Philip forgot about feeling mean, and just felt glad. Glad that Jane had not died, glad that he had made her laugh, glad that she was coming home tomorrow, and that when she did, he would have a marvellous present to give her.

16
Children in the Foliage

After school next day, Philip waited for Susan, who had asked to be excused hockey practice, at the station, and they walked up the hill together. Mrs Forbes, at breakfast time, had seemed doubtful about Jane's being allowed home, and had given them instructions that they were to come again to her house, if their own should be locked on their return. But Susan said confidently, 'If Jane has decided to come home, she will. She's very determined, and she hates sleeping out of her own bed. It's why I'm having so much trouble persuading her to come with me to Tiree.' And sure enough, when they came up the path, the outer door of *The Mount* was open, and they found Jane in the dining-room, sitting in her chair by the fire. Her injured arm was in a sling, and the black eye which Philip had predicted had indeed developed remarkably, staining the whole socket of her eye a deep, rich purple, and extending to her hair-line in two directions.

'Coo,' exclaimed Philip approvingly. 'What a beauty!'

'It's flattering to know that I have something you admire so much,' replied Jane dryly, but Philip knew that she was still amused, only probably too weary to show it.

She did, in fact, look very tired and ill, and Susan, whose delight in seeing her was tempered by painful anxiety, went and knelt on the floor beside her.

'Jane, please don't worry,' she said earnestly. 'We'll do everything. I'll cook, and do the shopping, and Philip will wash up, and—'

But Jane gently cut her short. With her good hand, she touched Susan's face in an unaccustomed gesture of affection, and said firmly, 'My dear, you don't have to worry either. You don't have to cook, and you don't have to shop. Jo is here. She's in the kitchen, and she's going to stay and look after us for as long as is necessary. Look—here she is now.'

The door from the kitchen opened, and a tall, large-boned woman in a blue overall came unhurriedly into the room. She was carrying some cutlery, which she put down on the end of the table. Philip had never seen Jo Wilcox before, because he had always been at school when she came, but she was not at all the Jo of his imagining, a typical, small, round, bustling Glasgow wifie. The real Jo was very different, a woman of the Islands, with pale red hair and clear, sea bird's eyes in a smooth, untroubled face. Philip knew that she was older than Jane, but there was an ageless quality about her which Jane did not have, and great strength, which relieved him. All day he had been worrying quietly about how he and Susan were to care properly for the frail invalid that Jane had suddenly become.

Susan jumped to her feet, and ran to hug the newcomer, saying, 'Jo, what a lovely surprise! Are you really going to stay and look after us? That will be marvellous!'

A pleased pinkness rose on Jo's fair cheeks as she returned Susan's embrace, but there was some severity in her lilting Highland voice as she replied, 'I shall stay, of course. When people are foolish, and will not wear their spectacles, and are run over by motor-cycles because they cannot see the traffic lights, it appears they need some sensible person to look after them.'

Jane sighed.

'This is going to be terrible,' she remarked to Philip. 'I don't suppose I shall ever be allowed outside again without a guide dog.'

Philip decided that this was intended as a joke, and was preparing to laugh, when he saw Jo looking at him, and decided against it.

'And you will be Philip North,' she said.

'Yes, I will,' Philip confirmed.

Jo looked him over without haste, then she looked at Jane, and shook her head.

'I cannot believe it,' she said.

'It is—very extraordinary,' Jane agreed. 'When he came at first, I could hardly bear to look at him, but now—I like it.'

'Indeed,' said Jo, 'it could be yourself and Master Hamish standing here again. Except, of course, that Master Hamish would never have worn such trousers, and that Susan will never be as beautiful as you, Miss Jane.'

'That will do, Jo,' said Jane, with a feeble attempt at repressiveness, while Susan smirked, and Philip carefully avoided catching her eye.

'Ah, well,' said Jo, terminating the interview in a queenly fashion, 'I have not all day to stand here talking to you. I must be getting back to my cooking. It will be my Hebridean fish pie this evening, and a nice rice pudding.'

As the kitchen door closed behind her, a look of horror crossed Jane's face.

'Oh, Lord,' she groaned. 'I hadn't thought of that. We'll be eating God's Bountiful Provision every single day. Oh, *Lord!*'

Susan couldn't help laughing, but she said sympathetically, 'Never mind, Jane. You can hide yours under your pillow, and I'll sneak in with a polythene bag, and winkle it out to the dustbin when she's not looking.'

'It's very good of you,' replied Jane wearily, 'but not the most practical way to dispose of rice pudding. I suppose I shall have to assert my authority—at least it will be a way of finding out whether I have any.' She moved uncomfortably in her chair, and added, 'If no one minds, I think I'll take to my bed now. I feel quite ridiculously weak.' For the first time, she looked really distressed, and there was a tremor in her voice as she said, 'I am so very sorry to be causing you all this trouble. I can't think how I could have been so stupid.'

'You weren't stupid,' Philip assured her. 'Lots of people have accidents. We're just thankful you didn't do yourself some awful damage that couldn't be repaired, aren't we, Sue?'

Susan nodded.

'I'll come with you, Jane, and help you into bed,' she said.

'Will you?' Momentarily Jane seemed doubtful, but then she said, 'Yes, please—I'd like that. But first—Philip, dear, do you suppose you could give me a hand up? Age doesn't come alone, and I'm as stiff as an old nag.'

'Sure,' agreed Philip easily.

He bent down to the left of the chair, put his shoulder where she could lean on it, and his arm firmly around her waist. Then, carefully, he raised her to her feet.

Jane thanked him, and transferred her hand to Susan's shoulder. Philip watched them move slowly across the room together, and disappear through the hall. Susan was gone for a long time. She never told anyone what she said to Jane when they were alone that afternoon, nor what Jane said to her, but after that, when they were together, they always had the look of people who had arrived at a place where they wanted to be.

Later that night, when Jo was in the kitchen, and Susan in her room doing her homework, Philip retrieved the piece of locket which he had found from his sock drawer, and went down to call on Jane. He had never been in her room before, and it surprised him just as much as Susan's had. The carpet and the curtains were blue, the walls pale grey, and there was hardly any furniture in it apart from the high, old-fashioned bed where Jane was lying, with a lot of pillows at her back.

'Oh, it's you, Philip,' she said, as he put his bright head round the door. 'Come in, my dear.'

Philip went and stood beside her, leaning against the edge of the bed in a friendly fashion. Jo had tilted the shade of the lamp so that the light would not shine into Jane's eyes, and they looked at each other through a pleasant dimness.

'I'm glad you've come,' Jane said. 'I hoped you would. I want to thank you. You've been so good—indeed, this whole tiresome business would have been a thousand times worse, if you hadn't been here to help us. Susan told me how kind you were to her yesterday, and as for myself—' the ghost of last night's laughter hovered tantalising about her lips '—well, when you left me, nothing seemed quite as dreadful and frightening as it did before you came. I'm very, very grateful.'

Philip was dumbfounded by the warmth of this unaccustomed praise. He felt his face going scarlet, but for once he didn't mind. Presently he found a voice, and said, rather gruffly, 'I didn't come to be thanked. But thanks, anyway. I came to give you a present.'

'A present?' Instantly Jane looked suspicious. 'It isn't a spider, is it? Or a mouse?'

Philip laughed, and remembered that long ago she had been a little girl in this house, with three brothers who looked like him.

'Would you be terrified?' he wanted to know.

'No, but I wouldn't be overwhelmed with gratitude, either.'

'Well, it's nothing like that. It's this.'

He had seen the half of the locket which she had given to Susan when he came in, lying on a small table beside her bed. Now he took his half out of his trouser pocket, and held it out to her. Her long, dry fingers closed over it, then curled back slowly, and she stared in rich astonishment into the palm of her own hand. It was as dramatic a reaction as Philip could have hoped for.

'My dear boy,' she said at length, 'where on earth did you find this?'

Philip told her, explaining how the floorboards of the summer house had come adrift, so that now you could put in your hand, where once the boards would have lain quite snugly against one another.

'It didn't occur to me until last night that it was yours,' he said, 'or I'd have given it to you when I found it. It was when the bit you gave to Susan fell out of the envelope, I saw it was the other half of the bit I'd found.'

'Yes, I see. Do you know,' said Jane, 'I had no idea that that was where I had lost it.' She reached out, and lifted from the table the piece of locket with the chain attached to it. Philip watched as she laid the two ovals side by side on the pale blue duvet, touching them wonderingly with her veined, ringless hand. 'I can scarcely believe it,' she told him. 'It must be nearly fifty years.'

'Yes, I know.' Philip leaned over, and pointed to the undamaged photograph, the one of the smiling young man. 'Is that Ewan MacNeill?' he asked bluntly.

Susan would have been aghast at such tactlessness, but Jane was not one to look for tact in a boy of Philip's age. All the same, her stunned silence made him fearful that he had offended her. He was opening his mouth to say he was sorry, when she turned her head and looked at him, with an expression in which there was perhaps a shade of irritation, but far more of surprise, and an anxiety that was not for herself at all, but for him.

'Dear me,' she sighed, 'is there no end to the telling of old tales?' But then, as usual, she went on to answer his question directly. 'No. That's Hamish, my younger brother. I'd have thought you might have recognised him—you're very alike. He gave me the locket on my eighteenth birthday. Ewan MacNeill's photograph was in the piece you found.'

Suddenly, Jane bit her lip, lay back on her pillows, and closed her eyes. The unbruised part of her face was very white. Philip looked at her nervously.

'Jane, I'm sorry,' he said. 'I'm tiring you too much. I'll push off now.'

But, rather feverishly, she detained him.

'No, Philip,' she begged, taking hold of his sleeve with a kind of tired urgency. 'Please don't go. I'm all right. It's just that something awful has occurred to me. Oh, Philip, are you and Susan making yourselves unhappy over me and Ewan MacNeill? Because you mustn't, really you mustn't. Ewan MacNeill has been dead for nearly half a century. What shocks me is to discover that there's anyone alive, apart from Jo and me, who even remembers his name. It's all wrong that children should grieve about something that was over and done with, before even their parents were born. Brooding about the past is for old people, and even they should be ashamed of themselves. I know I am, but—but—'

'Do you think about the past a lot?' Philip asked her.

'Yes, I'm afraid I do. I can't help it.' She was not asking for sympathy, only trying to explain what she regarded as a weakness. 'I think—if you have led the kind of life I have led, and have been so much alone at the end of it—it's almost impossible not to live more in the past than in the present. But, thank God—' she gave him the best smile she could manage '—having you and Susan here has prevented me from crossing the line to where I might not know the difference.'

Philip said, 'I thought I bothered you.'

'Bothered me?' said Jane. 'Oh, you bothered me for a very long time. I used to dread meeting you in the street with your mother, the sight of you pained me so much. And when you came here first—although I wouldn't have dreamed of refusing to have you—I felt as if a ghost had come out of the past to haunt me. However, I soon realised that you're far too much your own man to have an identity confused with anyone else's. Now, you seem to fit into my life very naturally.' She rested herself for a moment or two, then added, 'But you must promise me that you and Susan will forget about my past. It's dear of you to care, but at your age you should only be thinking about your own good future.'

'But it was so unfair, what happened to you,' Philip cried, in a sudden outburst of childish anger. 'About the ring. So unfair, Jane!'

'Oh, dear.' For the first time, she gave him a glance of open affection. 'You know about that too, do you? What a tender heart you have. Well, I admit it didn't seem very fair to me either, at the time. But now—perhaps we should all remind ourselves that it happened long, long ago.'

She lay still, with her eyes closed, and Philip wondered whether he should slip quietly away. But before he could make up his mind, she spoke again.

'How strange, though, that the locket should have been

109

in the old summer house. So many games of hide and seek. We used to play there endlessly when we were young, Will and Tom and Hamish and I, and the Guthrie children, and Ewan and his sister Sarah. I haven't been in that part of the garden for years. Frankly, I don't think I could bear it. You see, for me, it's in the garden that the past still lives—still seems to have a presence outside time. This house is dead now, but there I would hear their voices—Hamish, Tom, Ewan . . . Oh, Ewan . . . '

Philip was not sure that she was still talking to him, nor was he sure that he understood properly what she said next. He only knew that it reminded him of the story Susan had once told him, of Jane walking away from the little children who were laughing in the chestnut tree.

'Sudden in a shaft of sunlight
Even while the dust moves
There rises the hidden laughter
Of children in the foliage
Quick now, here, now, always—
Do you remember this poem, Hamish?
Ridiculous the waste sad time
Stretching before and after.
No, no, of course not. You're too young. Far too young.'

Philip touched her hand.

'Jane,' he said, 'I'm going now. I know what it was like for Dad. Ill people shouldn't have to talk too much.'

She had been speaking to Hamish, but when she came back, she knew that he was Philip.

'Well, perhaps not,' she agreed. 'But I'm glad we talked. And I'm glad you're here. Good night, my dear. Thank you for the present.'

'You're very welcome. Good night, Jane.'

Philip closed the door quietly behind him, and began the ascent of the mysterious night stairs. Susan would have left the light on for him on the little landing far above, but even so, as he mounted into that great, dark silence, the usual chill finger of disquiet touched his heart. As he passed the first floor landing, once again he saw the clear blade of

110

light shining under the door of that strangest of rooms, where no light should ever be.

'"This house is dead now."' He repeated Jane's words to himself as he climbed. '"This house is dead now." Oh, glory. If that's what she really thinks, it's a mercy she doesn't know the half of it.'

17

Jo Remembers

Jane spent most of the next two weeks in bed, recovering from her injuries, and being alternately spoiled and ordered about by Jo. Jo was barely a year older than Jane, but treated her exactly as she did Susan and Philip, as if her role were to be at the same time both sergeant-major and benevolent nanny. Jane was only too glad to let Jo take the responsibility for house and children away from her for a while; she was more badly hurt than she had herself realised at first, for the bruising on her face was like the tip of an iceberg, and it would be a long time before she could move without pain. And yet everyone who came to see her—Mrs Forbes, Professor Watkins, the young motor-cyclist and his mother, Dr Matheson and Nurse Brown from the Health Centre—went away puzzled, as well as relieved. For while to the casual eye she looked like a plain old woman with a bruised face and a helpless arm, anyone who looked closely could see that she was shining with some intense inner happiness.

For the first two days after Jane came home from the hospital, Susan and Philip were at school, but on Friday they both began a week's half-term holiday, and announced that they were going to spend it helping to look after Jane. The 'looking after' mostly took the form of sitting in her room, teaching her to laugh again, but, once started, she learned very quickly. There were hilarious games of *Monopoly* and *Scrabble*—in which both Jane and Susan seemed to think that Philip was spelling the words wrongly on purpose— and much of the merry, light-hearted conversation which can only take place when people are completely at ease with one another.

Philip, with the memory of his father's illness still fresh, was perhaps a wiser nurse than Susan. He knew when Jane was tired, and needed to be left to rest for a while, whereas Susan would have stayed with her every minute of the day. So, if he had an errand for Jo, he took Susan with him, and risked meeting Russ Cawley in Blantyre Road, and the remarks which would pursue him if he did. It was very cold out of doors, for the first severe frost of the winter had come early; by day the trees and shrubs in the garden sparkled in stiff white elegance under a pale blue shell of sky, while at dusk the paths and pavements were a myriad strewing of tiny stars.

One afternoon, Jane gave Philip a small parcel and a letter, and asked him to take them in to town, to Mappin and Webb, the jewellers in St Vincent Street.

'I want to have the locket repaired,' she told him, 'and if I have to wait until my Resident Dragon allows me to go myself, that may be a very long time. But see that they insure it properly, Philip, and bring me back the certificate —because of you, it has become a doubly precious possession.'

Philip was, perhaps for the first time ever, completely content with his place in life. He was aware that nothing was yet resolved; there was a future to be planned, and a great, unsolved mystery hanging in the background of the present; perhaps tests of courage lay ahead, and Philip was not at all sure how much courage he had. Nor did the pains and problems of his own brief past disappear. But, just for this one week, which he was spending in the company of someone who accepted him and needed him, each day was enough.

Only once did his confidence falter, and then very briefly. It was on the Wednesday of half-term week, when he had been helping Jo in the kitchen, Susan having gone out on an errand of her own. Jo had sent Philip with Jane's lunch tray; evidently she had managed to assert her authority, since she appeared to be living on cups of Marmite and occasional eggs, just as she usually did. When he came through the door, he found Susan already in the room, and Jane's duvet adrift with coloured holiday brochures. Obviously some friendly discussion had been taking place for a while before his arrival.

Philip stood in the doorway, and a wave of jealousy so strong that it shook him physically, broke over him. Already, they were planning what they would do together when he was no longer there. They couldn't even wait until he was out of the house. But before he had time to feel hurt, and left out, and miserable, Susan jumped to her feet and said, 'Here he is now, Jane. Will you ask him, or shall I?'

'Darling, he may not want to,' cautioned Jane.

But Susan said, 'Of course he'll want to. Philip, listen. Jane's getting bored enough with her own bed to think she might be able to endure a few nights out of it. So we're going to have our holiday next summer, after all. And we were wondering—do you suppose that you and your Mum might like to come with us? We thought we would go to Tiree, or maybe Mull, but anyway—we're agreed that it just wouldn't be half the fun without you. So, will you ask your Mum, Philip?'

Philip came into the room, and put down the tray on Jane's bedside table, his face rosy with pleasure. But it was to Jane he spoke, not Susan.

'Do you really mean Mum too?' he asked her.

'Definitely,' replied Jane.

'Then yes, thanks. I know she'll want to,' Philip said.

He had written to his mother at the weekend, a passionate letter in which he had let concern for spelling go to the winds, telling her about Ewan MacNeill, the gardener's son who had wanted to marry—he had almost said a princess. But the point was that the princess had wanted to marry the gardener's son. And he was sure that when she received it, his mother would want to see old wrongs righted, as much as he did.

On the Friday morning of half-term week, Susan and Philip were toiling uphill from the shops in Blantyre Road, bent under the burden of the week's household shopping. Jane had been wrong in saying that they would not have to shop, since Jo held that there was no point in keeping dogs, and barking yourself.

'I bet Miss Jane and Master Hamish never had to heave great bags of tatties up the hill from Barclay's,' complained Philip, as he laid down his plastic carriers on the pavement, and rubbed his aching arms. 'I bet they went for them in a Rolls Royce. I'm telling you, it's OK for some. You know, I think I'd like to wear an Academy cap, and jessy knickerbockers, and talk posh, and be called "Master Philip" by Jo. Sounds good, don't you think? "Yes, Master Philip. Right away, Master Philip."'

This speech conjured up a vision which caused Susan to giggle merrily, but she said, 'Nothing doing, I'm afraid. You can wear what you like, but you couldn't talk posh to save yourself. And while Jo would probably love to call you "Master Philip", our Miss Jane would have a fit. She doesn't like being called "Miss Jane" all that much. She thinks that everybody in the world is equal, you see. She doesn't even approve of the Queen.'

There was more giggling about this, but the mention of Master Hamish Gilmore led the conversation on to less mirth-provoking matters. With one thing and another, two weeks had passed since they had last had time to think of him, and his extraordinary treachery in the matter of Ewan MacNeill's letter. The strange room they now never mentioned at all, perhaps in the hope of convincing themselves that it was no longer any concern of theirs.

'I feel so awful, knowing what a stinker Hamish was,' said Philip. 'Jane thinks he was marvellous. She hardly ever mentions Will or Tom, but she talks about Hamish as if he was a real chum.'

'I know,' agreed Susan. 'The whole thing's weird. They used to write to each other once a month, and they must have done it for more than forty years.'

'Is he dead?' Philip asked.

'Oh, yes. They're all dead,' said Susan gloomily. They walked on in silence for a while, then she spoke again.

115

'Philip—I've been thinking—perhaps we should talk to Jo about this.'

'Not about the photographs?' cried Philip, who had been thinking about them.

'No, of course not. About the letter. You know how she loves to talk about Jane, and the old days. I just thought she might remember something—anything—that might help us to understand why Hamish didn't give Jane the package with the engagement ring.'

'I suppose we're sure it was the engagement ring?' said Philip cautiously.

'Oh, yes, it must have been,' said Susan. 'Think about the date. Third April, 1940. It fits in exactly with what my Dad told me, about Ewan being recalled early to his unit, and saying he would send the ring, before he went to France.'

Then Philip saw suddenly before his mind's eye an old bench in a tumbledown summer house, in a part of the garden which Jane could not bear ever to visit again. He remembered the initials, and the date carved on the seat: 'E.M. J.G. 31 MAR 40'. Susan was right. It all fitted. On the thirty first of March, Jane had agreed to marry Ewan. Three days later, in London, he had bought the ring, and, thinking that he was being careful, had sent it to his friend . . .

'Yes, all right,' Philip said. 'Let's ask Jo. It might do some good.'

Philip and Susan had arranged to play *Monopoly* with Jane that evening, but, just after supper, Professor Watkins turned up, carrying an alarming selection of convalescent reading for Jane. So the *Monopoly* had to be postponed. The two old friends were left alone with their coffee, and the children went into the kitchen with Jo. When the washing-up was finished, they took the opportunity offered, and Susan said, 'Jo, dear, we want to ask you something. When you worked here, when you were very

116

young, did you know our great uncle, Hamish Gilmore, at all well?'

Jo only ever needed an opening. A minute later, they were all sitting down, and her memory was spilling itself across the kitchen table.

'Master Hamish,' she said. 'Master Hamish was fourteen when I came to Glasgow in—let me see—nineteen thirty six, it must have been. I was sixteen, and Miss Jane was fifteen, a year older than Master Hamish. Did I know him well? I knew him well enough. He was a mischievous fellow, like most of his age—but he did love Miss Jane. They were like twins, these two, always laughing and whispering together, and I doubt a cross word ever passed between them.'

It was obvious to Susan from the general tone of these remarks that Jo had not known Hamish Gilmore well at all, and was only interested in him in as far as his behaviour had affected her blessed Miss Jane. She decided to try again, approaching the matter from Jo's more familiar angle.

'But you knew Jane better,' she prompted.

A softer look came into Jo's pale eyes.

'I knew her better,' she said, settling her elbows on the table, 'because she chose to make me her friend. When I came to this house from my home in Lewis, I had never been off the island before in my life, and I was homesick, and frightened half to death. I was terrified of the cook—a Mrs Wright, she was—and I could not understand the way people talked in Glasgow, we having the Gaelic at home, you see. And I thought nobody cared. Mrs Gilmore, Miss Jane's mother, was an English lady, very stern and remote, not sympathetic at all. The only time she ever spoke to me, except to give me an order, she told me that if I could not stop crying, she would have to send me back to my mother in Lewis, which of course made me cry all the more. And then, one afternoon, Miss Jane found me crying in the laundry room, when she came looking for her handkerchiefs, that I should have ironed, and had not. I thought she would be angry with me, too. But instead she

117

made me sit down, and she sat beside me, and put her arm round my shoulders, and asked me to tell her what was the matter. I can see her yet, as she was that day—like you she looked, Susan, although she was very beautiful, but wearing one of those brown gym tunics the High School girls had in those days, with her bonny black hair in a braid down her back. And I told her I was lonely, and I didn't have a friend. She said, "Well don't cry any more, Joanne. I'll be your friend." And she was true to her word. For all that she was a lady, and I was just a servant girl, never a day passed but she spoke to me, and often at night she would come up to my room, before she went to bed, and make me talk about the Island, and my home, and the folk I'd left. And three summers, before I met my Dan, she gave me money that she had saved out of her allowance, so that I could go home to Lewis to see my mother. She said she had no need of as much money as she had.' Jo looked over Philip's shoulder, as if she were seeing something very far away, and yet more real to her than many things close at hand. 'She was made for sunlight and love, that girl,' she said bitterly, 'and she had to spend her whole life doing her duty in darkened rooms.'

Philip began to understand why Jo felt about Jane the way she did, but he also saw Susan getting upset, so he decided to try to bring Jo to the point.

'Jo,' he said to her, 'we want to know about Ewan MacNeill.'

An expression of mingled sadness and disapproval crossed Jo's angular features.

'Ewan MacNeill was not worthy of her,' she said. 'He was only a gardener's son.'

Susan knew what she meant by this. Jo herself was a gardener's widow, and although one of her sons was a doctor, and the other a University lecturer, she thought of gardeners as her kind of people, not Miss Jane's. Philip had a sudden memory of his father, holding forth about how the Gilmores had exploited the poor, and it occurred to him that the problem was more complicated than his father had ever realised. He knew that if he said to Jo,

'Why did you allow the Gilmores to exploit you?' she would not have any idea what he was talking about. Only two things were clear. Jane had never expoited anybody, and Jane, as in so many things, would agree with his father.

Susan said gently, 'But she loved him, Jo.'

'She did so,' Jo agreed. 'They had played together in the gardens, as children will, and you cannot stop young people falling in love. The young MacNeill seemed to think the sun rose and set upon her, as well he might, and she—she never wanted anyone else, before or after. There were plenty of others she could have had—that old Professor at her bedside now, he was one of them—but it was Ewan MacNeill she loved, with his red cheeks and his bright blue eyes, and his hair that always looked as if he had just crawled through a hedge. He was the one she would have gone against her father for.'

'Are you saying he wasn't handsome?' asked Susan, who had been rather extravagant in her picturing of Jane Gilmore's lover. Jo probably sensed this, for she smiled indulgently at Susan—but, being Jo, strictly told the truth.

'I do not think anyone would have called him handsome,' she said, 'although he must have pleased Miss Jane well enough. He was little and thin and quick—she looked taller in those days, but he hardly came up past her shoulder—and he had a very cheeky face, which appealed more to Miss Jane than it did to her mother and father. He made her laugh, and that is a comforting thing to remember, for the poor girl had little to laugh about when he was gone. But oh, it was all so strange, what happened in the end.'

The smile had vanished from Jo's face, as Susan and Philip exchanged glances. Were they getting to the heart of the matter at last?

'You mean,' Susan prompted, 'that he didn't send the ring, when he said he would?'

Jo nodded wordlessly.

Philip said carefully, 'Jo, please. We want to ask you something. Just suppose that Ewan MacNeill had been

119

afraid to write to Jane directly, in case her father recognised his writing, and nabbed the letter—and suppose that he sent the letter to Hamish Gilmore instead. Can you think of any reason why Hamish Gilmore might not have given it to her—why he might have sided with his father, and not wanted Jane to marry Ewan at all?'

It took Jo a moment or two to work out what all this meant, but then she looked at Philip as if he had gone crazy.

'I cannot,' she said flatly. 'Where could you have got such an idea, Philip?' Then, realising that Miss Jane's favourite brother was under attack, she went on more vigorously, 'Master Hamish was the only one in the family both of them could trust. Ewan MacNeill and Master Hamish had been friends since their childhood, and as for Master Hamish and Miss Jane—well, have I not told you? They were devoted to each other.'

There was an uncomfortable silence in the kitchen, heated by Jo's smouldering indignation. But then Susan said, 'Jo, I'm sorry, but we don't think it could have been quite like that. You see, we found an old letter, in a box at Philip's house, and we think it proves that Hamish Gilmore did get the letter—and the ring. You'd better have a look at it.'

Jo, who at sixty-eight could still read perfectly well without glasses, scanned the letter which Philip put in front of her, and it was clear that any other feeling she might have had was swallowed up by sheer astonishment. There was another silence, broken only by the ticking of the old kitchen clock, which still hung on the wall beside the back door. Eventually, Jo said, 'It is his handwriting, the young MacNeill's.' Then she shook her head helplessly, and said, 'I still say it is impossible. Not Master Hamish.' She seemed to be at a loss for any other words.

'Jo,' pleaded Susan, 'please think. If you can't help us, we shall never get to the bottom of this mystery.'

'But you will never tell Miss Jane,' cried Jo, in sudden alarm. 'Promise me, Susan. I will not see her hurt again.

She loved Master Hamish, and she has had so few people to love.'

'Or who have loved her,' agreed Susan sombrely, 'and not just used her for their own ends. Don't worry, Jo. We don't want to see her hurt either. But—I don't know how to explain. Philip and I just feel that if we could get some clue to why Hamish Gilmore behaved as he did—so completely out of character, by all accounts—one day there might be something to tell Jane that would give her comfort, not pain.'

It was impossible, of course, to tell her of the empty room that was not empty, and the photographs, and the light that shone where no light should. She would have been outraged by such wicked nonsense—and was anyway interested in one thing only, protecting Jane.

Jo sat for a long time, staring bleakly into a past which Philip and Susan could scarcely imagine. They were just making up their minds that this was useless, and preparing to leave, disappointed, for their beds, when, very slowly, her expression began to change. Out of that remote region, the remembrance of half a century ago, something was coming back to her.

'There was an incident—concerning a letter,' she said. 'Wait, now. Let me think. Yes. I am beginning to remember.' Philip and Susan were afraid to look at each other. Dry-mouthed, they stared at Jo across the table until their eyes hurt, and they thought they might faint with fear—fear that, even now, she might not remember anything that mattered—if she remembered anything at all. But then she said, 'I do recollect. It was after Master Hamish went to Canada—and that must have been just after Ewan MacNeill was killed, because Miss Jane was distraught, and he did not want to leave her—but of course he had no choice. Well now, after he was gone, the other maid who was here at the time—a flighty creature, Dinah, or Dora, her name was—was set to turning out Master Hamish's room, for he would not be requiring it again in the immediate future. Mercifully, Miss Jane did not know at that time that he would never be requiring it

121

at all, for he did not come back to Glasgow after the War. And when the maid moved the chest of drawers, what did she find but a letter, addressed to Master Hamish, and never opened. We thought it had come while he was away in London for his interviews, and had been put on the chest of drawers for him to find when he came back. Well, maybe a draught had caught it, or it had slipped on the polished wood, but somehow it had fallen down, and got stuck between the skirting board and the back of the chest. I remember the girl brought it down to the kitchen, and said should she give it to Miss Jane to readdress. But Mrs Wright, who thought she was in charge of the world, said no—the correct thing to do was to take it to Master Hamish's father, and let him deal with it. And that was what was done. It was handed over to Mr Gilmore, of that I am certain. I doubt that I have ever thought of it again. It did not seem important at the time.' She sighed, and added, with another shake of her head, 'It must have been just after that that Miss Jane's troubles with her father began. He had the first of his illnesses that summer, and she had to nurse him through it, Mrs Gilmore herself being ill by that time. Some sort of brain fever, he had—the sort of thing you would get these antibiotics for nowadays, and recover in a fortnight. Oh, he recovered, all right, though not in a fortnight—he lived for another thirty years, and more. But that first illness affected him. He looked like a man who had seen a ghost, and Miss Jane told me afterwards there were things he could never remember. He would go around the house searching for something, but he would never tell her what it was. She said it fretted him. Many things fretted him, it seems to me.'

'But this explains everything,' said Susan, in a small voice. 'It was Jane's father who stole the ring, and Ewan's letter, not Hamish at all. Oh, I'm glad it wasn't Hamish! But poor, poor Jane.'

Jo was looking tired and haggard.

'Susan,' she said earnestly, 'please, promise me you will not bring this matter up with Miss Jane. She is tired and in pain, and even if it would please her to know that Ewan

MacNeill kept his word, she would have to know that her own father had done her the most terrible wrong. You and Philip have surely done the best deed of your lives—you have made her so happy, she feels that even she may have some future that is worth looking forward to. Do not make her wretched again by forcing her to recall the past. My dear, you cannot know what it was like.'

And Susan would have promised, for Jo's pleading was powerful, but it was Philip who spoke first, in words which amazed even him as he said them.

'All right. We shan't tell her anything for the moment. But we can't promise for ever, Jo. She'll have to know—when we find the ring.'

18

A Change of Direction

These were strong and dramatic words, but of course, when he was challenged by Susan later on that night, Philip was unable to say just how such a discovery was to be made. He knew as well as Susan did that old William Gilmore might have disposed of Jane's engagement ring in any number of ways. He might have sold it, or given it away, or tossed it into the heart of the drawing-room fire, or thrown it into the Clyde. The least likely thing was that he would have kept it, a constant reminder of his own cruel treachery. And yet—had not every clue, every thread of the mystery, so far, led back to the old tale of Jane Gilmore and her love for Ewan MacNeill? Would not the finding of the ring provide the only happy ending to that story that was possible now? And had not the letter, and the half locket, turned up, just as improbably, after nearly fifty years?

What Philip did not share with Susan, who had said over and over that she would never enter the strange drawing-room again, was his belief that the last clue, if not the ring itself, lay behind that mysterious first floor door, where the line of light now shone every single night. He did not know why he thought this, except that the mystery of the room was so obviously unfinished, and no other line of enquiry seemed open; moreover, there was something insistent about the light, something almost inviting. But when Philip thought of the drawn curtains they had seen from the road, and the awesome things they had already seen in the room by day, any such invitation was easy to resist; the idea of entering the place at night frightened him as much as it did Susan. And he wished fervently that he had not drawn his great grandfather and Jane, sitting by the drawing-room fire. He had tried to rub them out, but they seemed to be indelible.

Meantime, however, there were other, less eerie things to occupy one's mind. On Monday, Susan went rather reluctantly back to school, but Philip, because of a public holiday, had an extra day off. He had made up his mind that, in Susan's absence, he would use the opportunity of an hour alone with Jane, to consult her about the future. At the weekend, she had begun to get up for a while in the afternoons, and, although she was still stiff, and needed support for her arm, managed the move to her chair in the dining-room well, with Philip's help. So, on Monday, when he had helped her into her chair, and irritated her by insisting on spreading a rug over her knees, he said, 'I want to talk.'

'How unusual,' said Jane. 'What about?'

'Things,' said Philip.

Jane watched with mild envy as he seated himself in the chair opposite hers, and writhed his long legs into an incredible knot. But before he could start, she said suddenly, 'Oh, by the way, I meant to tell you. I've had the most extraordinary letter from your mother, apologising because she never knew that my young man's father was a welder in the shipyards at Clydebank. Neither did I, actually, but never mind.'

Philip went pink.

'Hell,' he growled irritably. 'That was my Grandpa North. She always gets everything wrong.'

'Does she, indeed?' said Jane, amused. 'I assumed she had been misinformed by you. However—she also says she hopes to see much more of me in future, and if that means I shall see much more of you, I'm all for it. Now, what did you want to talk about?'

Philip took a deep breath, and said, 'I want your advice. Jane, do you think I could be a scientist when I grow up?'

'A scientist?' This was clearly not what she had expected. 'I understood that you wanted to be a professional footballer.'

Now it was Philip's turn to look surprised.

125

'How do you know that?' he demanded.

'Mrs Cawley told me,' said Jane. 'She came to see me this morning, when you were out at the shops for Jo. She doesn't know how I can stand living in this house, and neither do I. And oh, Philip! She brought me the biggest box of chocolates I've ever seen in my life—quite horrible. It was so obviously her contribution to "Help the Aged", I didn't feel I could tell her I've loathed confectionery for as long as I can remember. But anyway, she stayed for two hours, drank endless cups of coffee, and told me a great deal about you and—Russell, is it?—including the fact that you both want to be professional footballers. She reckons his prospects of achieving this ambition are better than yours, although personally, I disagree with her.'

'Do you? Why?'

'Because,' replied Jane, with an old-ladyish tartness that startled Philip, 'if half of what she says about him is true, he'll almost certainly be in jail by the time he's sixteen.'

This was not comfortable talk.

'What did she tell you about me?' asked Philip cautiously.

'Well, let me see. She told me that you and Russell had always been great pals—what Mrs Cawley calls "real laddies", which I took to mean that you never did any work at school, and were responsible for most of the graffiti in the lifts at Maxie Court.'

Philip was mortified. This was dreadful, and not at all the kind of conversation he had intended.

'I thought you liked Mrs Cawley,' he said reproachfully.

'Oh, I do,' said Jane. 'But I don't think I'd like Russell very much. But let's not worry about that for the moment. Do I gather that you've changed your mind about being a footballer?'

'Yes,' said Philip, relieved. 'Yes, I think I'd rather be a scientist. The kind who wears a white coat, and looks down a microscope, like in *Dr Strangeglove and the Growth*.'

'Oh, I see. That kind,' said Jane faintly.

Philip watched her in fond exasperation. Honestly, he

126

thought, it was becoming as difficult to get her to keep her face straight as it used to be to get her to smile.

'Don't laugh, Jane,' he implored.

'I'm not laughing.'

This was so obviously untrue that he decided to ignore it, and, to recall her to the business in hand, said, 'I thought that since you're a scientist, you could tell me how to go about it.'

Jane leaned back in her chair, and tutted impatiently.

'My dear boy,' she said, 'once and for all, I am not a scientist. About a century ago, I did two years of Maths and Physics at Glasgow University, which hardly qualifies me as a scientist, or an adviser of aspiring scientists. But—come on, Philip. Tell me the truth. What put this idea into your head? I can't really believe it has anything to do with Dr Strangefingers, or Glove, or whatever you said.'

And of course, she was right. This was the opening Philip needed, but he was not sure that he could take it, even now. Not with her brown eyes suddenly looking at him so seriously. Slowly he unknotted himself, and flopped down on the hearthrug, so that he could sit with his back to her, leaning against the arm of her chair. Even then, it was hard to start. He could not tell her what he did not himself know, that it was living with her that had changed him; he thought the reason was something else, and did not realise that his feeling about that, too, had come to him through living with her. But eventually he said, 'I think it would please my Dad.'

Jane was silent for a moment, then she said carefully, 'Not the best of reasons. Why does it matter, now?'

Then it all began to come out.

'I couldn't get on with him, Jane.'

He could no longer see her face, but he felt her fingers fleetingly touch his hair.

'No,' she said calmly. 'I couldn't get on with mine either. I used to be very jealous of people who were really good friends with their fathers, and I used to think that if I wasn't, it must be my fault. I expect you think that too, don't you?'

'Yes.'

'Well, I don't—any longer—think that we should. You see, there's no real reason why we should love people, just because they happen to be related to us. We should love people who treat us with humanity, and respect our right to be ourselves, and grow as we choose. My father never thought his children had any rights, then when he was old, he couldn't understand why two of his sons emigrated, and the one who stayed in the same house was a complete stranger to him. As for yours—he would never have allowed me to get to know him well, but I remember him as a very touchy, difficult young man.'

Philip said, 'I annoyed him. I don't know why. I just did.'

'There's no mystery about that,' said Jane, 'if he really hated the Gilmores as much as he once told me he did. You are very like the male Gilmores, Philip—only, thank God, much nicer than most of them. You have a kindness in you that was lacking in them.'

'Maybe I get that from you.'

'You're not descended from me. I expect you get it from your mother. But the point I'm trying to make is that you don't have to feel guilty, because your father died. You should try to remember any happy days and good things you shared with him, and hold onto these as you grow up, but beyond that . . . We have to live with the past as it was, Philip. Death doesn't change it, nor does wishing it had been different. It wasn't your fault. And your future belongs to you, not to your father. So if you want to be a footballer, be a footballer. But if you want to be a scientist, want it for yourself, not for anyone else.'

Philip thought about this, and comfort began to flow into him. He said, 'I still think I'd like it, Jane. If you think I could.'

He squirmed round on the rug, hugging his knees, and looked up at her. But she returned his gaze with an expression which reminded him of the bad days, before he had taught her to smile. She seemed to be trying to make up her mind whether to say something, or not, but must

128

eventually have decided to risk speaking her mind.

'Philip,' she said, 'I think you could be anything in the world you want to be—on one condition.'

'What's that?'

'That you stop allowing Russell Cawley to decide how you live your life. I'm sorry, my dear. It's no affair of mine, and I know better than most people that we must take our friends where we can find them. But—at the risk of sounding old maidish and stuffy—if you don't stop fooling around soon, you will waste an excellent intelligence, and in the end may achieve as little as Russell Cawley ever will. Even his mother admits this. She told me this morning that Russell had no brains, but that she worried about you.'

Philip thought it as well to be honest.

'I don't have to give him up,' he told her. 'He's giving me up. He says I've got posh since I came here to live.'

This did bring the smile back to Jane's eyes.

'Have you really?' she said, observing his rumpled head and grubby denims. 'I hadn't noticed. You look exactly the same to me. Anyway—don't grieve too much. You'll make other friends.'

'Yes. But I feel bad, Jane. He's always been my chum, ever since we were in Primary One. I don't like the Cawleys thinking we've fallen out because of Wisteria Avenue, and your father being Lord Provost of Glasgow. You should understand that. Susan says you think everyone is equal.'

'I don't think anything of the sort,' said Jane indignantly. 'That would be a very stupid thing to think, when it so obviously isn't true. What I think is that everyone should start out in life with the same opportunities, so that all the wicked old divisions that made relationships so difficult for my generation—based on where you lived, and who your father was, and your accent, and which school you went to—can finally be blown sky high. What people do with opportunities is a different matter. Russell Cawley—who is a very privileged young man, it seems to me—will do nothing with those he has already. But I'm relieved beyond measure to hear that you want to do something with yours. I don't believe the rest of the Cawleys will hold it against you.'

For a moment, Philip's relief was also beyond measure, but then it was swamped by misgiving.

'Oh, Jane,' he cried, 'it's too late! I can't do Maths.'

This did not seem to alarm her terribly.

'Oh, fiddlesticks,' she replied coolly. 'Any fool can do Maths. I'll teach you, if you like. But only if you really mean to work. I'm getting old, and I don't think I'd have the energy nowadays to push you, if you lost interest.'

Philip could scarcely believe his ears.

'Would you honestly?' he said. 'I would work hard.'

'Right, then,' she said easily, as if she were not offering very much. 'Three afternoons a week, for an hour after school, and we'll see how we get on. Give me another week or two, because to tell the truth I still feel a bit done up, but after that, we'll get going.' She smiled at him, and added simply, 'It will give me great pleasure if I can help you. Sometimes I've felt sad and bitter because I had to waste so much of my own life, and if I can see you happy, and making something good out of yours, it will make up to me for a great deal.'

This made Philip feel inadequate again.

'But, what if I let you down?' he whispered.

Jane leaned forward in her chair, and gave him a friendly push which sent him rolling on his back on the hearth rug.

'What an ass you are,' she said. 'How could you possibly let me down? I only want to enjoy you, not to own you. I don't really care what you do, as long as you're happy. Put it this way. If you take a degree, I'll come to your graduation. If you become a professional footballer, I'll come to Hampden to see you play. If I live long enough.'

'You had better,' said Philip fiercely.

'I'm in the mood to make the effort,' replied Jane.

They sat together for a while, in the silence which Philip had once found so irritating, but now accepted as a pleasant part of life. He used it to think for a bit, and at length said, 'Jane, may I ask you a question?'

'Only one,' she said firmly. 'Then we are going to have our tea, and after that you will kindly do your strong man act, and help me back to my bed.'

'Yes, all right. I was wondering—why didn't you run away?'

'Run away?' Jane sounded mystified. 'When should I have run away?'

'When your father wouldn't let you stay at University.'

'Oh. My father again.' For a moment, he thought he had annoyed her, but if he had, her annoyance was fleeting. Patiently, she gave him the only answer she knew. 'It would have been impossible. You see, in those days you needed some money of your own to run away with, and I had none. My allowance was stopped when I refused to come to heel over Ewan MacNeill, and by the time I got it back, I was far too tired and dispirited to run anywhere.'

'Your brothers did.'

'Yes, indeed, and no one could have blamed them. But it wouldn't have been right for me. Oh, Philip—I've never talked about these things to anyone, and it's very difficult—but I'll try to tell you, if only because you seem to know so much already. My father was a harsh, unforgiving man, but—although he made it impossible for me to love him, and although I suspect he once did me a most cruel wrong—underneath all his sound and fury, he was such a disturbed, miserable creature. He needed me. I don't believe in running away. I believe we should try to be brave, and not moan. I don't know anything else but that. Now go, and ask Jo to put the kettle on—and please, dear boy, no more difficult questions today.'

19

The Man Who Saw Ghosts

Now the days began to pass very quickly, like beads slipping off a string. It was dark in the afternoon, tinsel bells and streamers appeared in the shops, and holly wreaths were hung up outside the florist's in Blantyre Road. Philip was cast as Widow Twankey in his school's Christmas pantomime, *Aladdin,* a performance to which Jane was looking forward with childlike relish, and satisfaction that with her new spectacles she would actually be able to see the stage. By the first week in December she was on the way to recovery, although Dr Matheson was still insisting that she should get up late and go to bed early, and do no cooking or other work in the house until after New Year. This would have irked her badly, had not Professor Watkins just completed a new book; she was very busy reading the manuscript, and gleefully querying his calculations in her red notebook. Philip's Maths lessons were under way; he found Jane a patient but strict teacher, who gave him so much homework that sometimes he was upstairs in the evening for almost as long as Susan.

Philip's mother was due home on the eighteenth of December. He was looking forward to seeing her, but could not disguise from himself the pain he would feel when he had to leave *The Mount* and his friends there for the lonely little house in Tarbet Gardens. But then, one day, something unexpected and marvellous happened. He learned, in a letter from his mother, that she had arranged for him to stay with Jane whenever she was on night duty at the hospital. This would be one week in three, and occasionally other weekends. Susan was beside herself with delight, and so, less exuberantly, was Philip.

'But are you sure you don't mind?' he asked Jane, who was sitting at the dining-room table, with Professor Watkins' manuscript spread out in front of her. She looked at him incredulously over her half-moon glasses.

'Mind?' she repeated. 'Of course I don't mind. I've been wondering for weeks how I could possibly get along without you. Now I shall always know you'll soon be coming back.'

And so the days went by in great contentment, with only that line of uncanny light under the drawing-room door to remind the children that all questions had not been answered, and that there was one unfinished piece of business to which they might possibly attend.

It was a question of courage, of course. Susan said, quite frankly, that she didn't believe she could ever go into that place again, by day or night, after the terrifying afternoon when they saw the portrait of the Gilmore children. Philip was determined that he would go in, but he too was afraid, and it was easier to keep shelving the decision, concentrating on other matters, until, at last, time had almost run out. Philip didn't tell lies to himself; he knew in his heart that if he could not summon the courage to open the door before he left for home, he never would on a later visit. And he also knew that if he did not, he would have failed the bravest person he was ever likely to know. It was this awareness which made him go through to Susan's room, on the last Friday afternoon—his mother was to return on Monday—and say, as firmly as he could, 'Sue, I've made up my mind. I'm going into that room tonight. Are you going to come with me?'

'No,' said Susan.

'All right. I don't blame you. I'll go myself.'

Susan was sitting on the side of her bed, unpacking her school bag. She looked at Philip with eyes dark and wide with apprehension, and said quaveringly, 'You don't really mean it, do you?'

'Yes, I do.' Philip sat down on the bean bag, and said,

133

with a certain amount of embarrassment, 'I'll do it for Jane. She's done a hell of a lot for me, and I want to do something for her. I'm sure the clue to where that ring is must be in that room. I'm going to find it, and give it to her.'

'You gave her back her precious locket,' Susan reminded him, pleadingly. 'Isn't that enough?'

'No. That didn't cost me anything.'

Susan looked at Philip in some awe. She scarcely could believe that this was the same person as the bad-tempered, self-absorbed boy who had come here so unwillingly only twelve weeks ago. And of course she knew that it was Jane who had changed him, just as he had changed Jane. Then Susan remembered how much she too loved Jane, and thought she would not like to be outdone in courage and generosity.

'All right,' she said in a whisper. 'I'll come. But I'm very scared, Philip.'

'So am I. We'd be fools if we weren't,' said Philip. 'But I think we'll be all right—and God, I'll be glad to have you there, Sue.'

'Do you think we'll see a ghost?' asked Susan fearfully.

Philip hesitated before he answered this. He didn't want to scare Susan so much that she would change her mind about coming with him; at the same time, it would be silly to fob her off with assurances that all they were likely to see—again—was the furniture they had seen the last time. She was a very intelligent girl, and he knew that she knew better than that. Probably it was better simply to tell her the conclusions he had arrived at—for he had thought long and seriously about the whole affair.

'Yes, I think it's very likely,' he said. 'As you yourself said, the drawn curtains suggest a room that is—or was—lived in. Someone pulled the curtains—but not the night we saw them pulled, of course. Everything that's happened in that room makes me think that we're seeing things as they were long, long ago.'

'But not before the nineteen twenties,' Susan pointed out. 'In the portrait of the children, Jane looked about eight or nine.'

'Exactly,' Philip agreed. 'I'm sure that afternoon we saw the room as it was when Jane was young. It all comes back to Jane. Sue—' Philip paused again, trying to put his thoughts in order '—do you remember once asking me if I thought the light was there when we weren't looking at it?'

'Yes.'

'Well, there isn't any way of knowing that, of course. But thinking about that led me on to realise something else. It hasn't got anything to do with us seeing it—it has to do with Jane thinking it. On the night when she came home, after having the accident, I talked to her for a while. She told me that she thinks a tremendous amount about the past—she was all apologetic, as if she could help it, poor old thing. She also said this house was dead. But we know it isn't. I believe the past comes to life when Jane thinks about it, and that what we're seeing is her—well, thought, or dream, call it what you like. And I reckon she thinks plenty about what went on in that room.'

To his relief, Susan took this much more calmly than Philip had expected. She nodded her dark head pensively.

'Yes,' she agreed. 'And she isn't thinking about furnishings, either. She's thinking about people.' She sat very still on her bed for a while, then she said, 'You know, it would seem preposterous, if this was a bungalow in Nairobi, or your place in Tarbet Gardens. But in this house, anything seems possible, doesn't it? What about the camera?'

Philip shrugged his shoulders.

'That's something else, isn't it?' he replied. 'I think you've just given the only answer. In this house, anything seems possible. I sometimes think everything in it has a memory. That's what makes it so—so—what's the word?'

'Oppressive,' said Susan.

Perhaps it was as well, in a way, that Jo had decided that Jane was looking tired, and had ordered her to bed before supper. Nowadays, Jane was more observant of the children than she used to be, and would probably have noticed their white faces and lack of appetite. When they went into her room to say good night to her, she was already half asleep, and seemed not to see that Susan was more wan, and Philip less perky than usual.

'We'll go up, and have our baths, and get ready for bed,' said Philip, as they went upstairs. 'Then we'll have a game of chess. We don't want to do this while Jo is still prowling around.'

'She'll have gone to bed by ten,' said Susan. 'Fortunately, she's sleeping in the old nursery, at the back of the house.'

'Yes,' said Philip. 'We'll come down then.'

They prepared for bed, put on their dressing-gowns, and pushed the pieces around on the chess board, stupidly, not caring who won. Philip wondered whether they should arm themselves with weapons—the brass candlestick had served the purpose once—but decided not. Whatever they had to encounter that night, it was nothing that could be fought with physical strength. The strength they needed must be mental, and whether they had enough of it remained to be seen. They waited until they heard the church clock of St Kentigern's striking ten, then, without a word, they tiptoed downstairs. With Susan clinging feverishly to his sleeve, Philip opened the drawing-room door. On an intake of breath, they slid round it, and pressed their backs to the solidity of its inner side.

They had not known what to expect; they never could have imagined that what they would see would be beautiful—so beautiful that fear flowed from them with their breathing out, and they stared spellbound. Through a steady, lambent light, they saw the room where old William Gilmore had kept his treasures, which Philip had so strangely painted, and which Jane Gilmore had redrawn in her imagination, night after night, as she lay sad and sleepless in her bed downstairs. At first, it was like a photograph, a scene caught as the camera clicks; fine furniture, good paintings, rich curtains, a prosperous man in late middle age reading in his chair by the fire, while his dark haired daughter sat curled up on the fender, with her Siamese cat in her lap. Philip had drawn them, and there they were.

But then, even as the children gazed, it seemed that the camera began to roll. Suddenly the fire leaped up, the shadows danced, and William Gilmore leaned forward in his chair to speak to Jane. They could not hear what he said, but Jane rose at once, pushing her cat gently onto the floor. She was lithe and upright in her grey silk dress, and as beautiful as in an old servant's memory, as she moved towards the bedroom door in the corner of the room. The tiny cat ran after her, rubbing itself lovingly against her ankles, and they were gone. The door closed behind them, and Philip heard Susan sigh.

What happened next, for Jane, remained for half a century speculation, an aching suspicion which was fuelled, in later years, by the deranged mutterings of a sick old man, but never really proved. Whereas now Philip and Susan saw, and judged.

William Gilmore got up from his chair, and went over to the door which Jane had just closed. It was as if the portrait in the dining-room, which had so disturbed Philip and Susan, had suddenly come to life. Its energy released, they understood how, in life, he had dominated his environment, and why Jane had stopped being nervous when he died. He was even taller than the portrait suggested, a broad, powerful giant, bald-headed, red-faced, blue-eyed and—at this moment—furtive. He made sure that the door was properly shut, then he came back and sat down again, taking from the inside pocket of his jacket a long, white envelope, which he turned over thoughtfully in his thick hands. Then, very quickly, he tore it open, taking from it a sheet of writing paper and another envelope, smaller than the first, but bulky. He unfolded the sheet of paper, read what was written on it, tore it in two and dropped it contemptuously on the carpet. Perhaps he battled with his conscience just a little before he turned his attention to the other envelope, but, if he did, it was not for long. He opened it, took out a small white box, glanced at its contents with irritation, and put it on the arm of his chair. Then, to the children's anguished indignation, he opened and read the last letter that Ewan MacNeill would ever write to Jane. He sat with it between his fingers for a long time, with his chin down on his chest, and his blue eyes staring into nothingness, while Susan and Philip waited, expecting that at any moment he would throw ring and letter into the fire. But he did not.

As if, all at once, he had made up his mind, he got to his feet, picked up the box and the letter, and walked across the room to his desk. There, under the grave eyes of his own four children, he found another envelope, into which he slipped the letter, and the little box containing the ring. When he had sealed it—it was Susan's turn to hear Philip sigh—he put it in the top right hand drawer of the desk, and locked it with a small key which he took from his waistcoat pocket. As he came back towards the fire, he saw the two pieces of Ewan's letter to Hamish lying where he had tossed them onto the floor. He picked them up, crumpled one in each hand, and threw them into the fireplace. One landed among the embers; it sent up a feeble spurt of flame, shrivelled, and was gone. The other fell in the hearth, and lay there unharmed. How it got from there to the box on the desk, and so to Philip's house, no one would ever know; perhaps Dora or Dinah, coming in the morning to clean out the grate, had rescued it. To Philip and Susan it didn't matter; there were deeper mysteries than that.

For a while, observed across fifty years by his great grand children, William Gilmore stood on the hearthrug, tossing the little key up and down on the palm of his hand. Then he did what only a man with a guilty secret would ever have done. Instead of putting the key back in his pocket, he stepped towards the fireplace, and slipped it into the narrow space between the looking glass and the wall, where the base of the glass rested on the chimney piece. For who would ever think of looking there?

And Philip and Susan would have hugged each other, and rejoiced—but before they had time to move, something dreadful happened. So far, the scene had been played out at the far end of the room, as on a cinema screen; it had been so engrossing that Susan and Philip had forgotten to be afraid, feeling that they were unseen spectators, not participants in the unfolding drama. But of course, there were two exits from this room, one through the bedroom, the other through the door onto the landing, against which they now stood. Their great grandfather had actually taken several steps towards them before they realised what was happening; he was almost upon them, making for the door, before their frozen limbs loosened, and Philip groped sideways, frantically, for the ebony handle. But it was too late. Very afraid, but also stern, angry and accusing, they forced themselves to stare up into his popping blue eyes, and in that instant, they knew. *He saw them.* An expression of stupid, vacant terror spread across his large pink face, which blanched as his mouth wordlessly opened and closed. And as he stood, unable to move, they did. Philip found the handle and wrenched open the door; pulling Susan after him, he ran out onto the landing, and the door swung soundlessly shut behind them.

This time, they did not collapse on the landing, and it was Susan, until now the passive partner, who kept her head and acted on instinct. On light, bare feet she leaped away from Philip up the attic stairs; when he caught up with her at the top, she was coming out of her room, clutching her father's camera, and the bundle of photographs, with their weird images of long ago.

'Quick!' she gasped. 'Your painting, Philip. Get your painting!'

It was the work of seconds to whip the painting out of its drawer; Susan snatched it and was off again. Down the long night stairs Philip followed her, through the hall and the dining-room, greenly lit by moonlight, and into the dark kitchen. The faint glow of smouldering embers guided Susan to the stove; seizing the poker, she levered open the little transparent door and rammed everything— camera, photographs and painting—into the fire. The painting made a little flame, but for the rest it was a blackening, and a melting, and a slow falling apart. When they went back upstairs, the light under the drawing-room door had gone out.

139

Ever afterwards, Susan and Philip believed that it was because they had been resourceful, and had destroyed these monstrous objects, that the light never shone again. But there might have been another explanation. Perhaps, that night, Jane Gilmore decided finally to step out from the shadow of the past, and turn her mind to present things.

Surprisingly, in the circumstances, both children slept long and dreamlessly. But in the early morning, when the silence of night was displaced by the first thin stirrings of a new day, Philip rose and went down alone to the cold, deserted drawing-room. And there he found the little gold key which his great grandfather had sought in vain all over the house, unable to tell his daughter what he was looking for, unable even to remember what he had lost.

20
Hidden Laughter

When he showed the key to Susan, before they went downstairs, Philip said, 'We'll go to my house and open the drawer after breakfast.' And Susan, who still had a faint look of bewitchment on her face, replied, 'Yes, of course.' But the day didn't work out so as to allow that.

Jo had had earache the previous day, hadn't slept, and got up looking ghastly. Jane, taking her revenge, ordered her back to bed with a peremptoriness which made Susan and Philip snigger in the larder. However much she had come to believe in equality in her old age, Miss Jane obviously had not forgotten how to give an order to a servant. But then, looking anxious, she went searching for some almond oil and aspirin, and put on the kettle for hot-water bottles.

As she filled them, Philip stood watching her. He saw her old and grey-haired, round-shouldered under her shabby black cardigan, still slightly lame after her accident. And suddenly, painfully, he remembered the tall, supple, beautiful Jane whom he and Susan had glimpsed last night, in a room strangely re-created by this old woman's memories. And the contrast brought fury surging up in him against that selfish, callous man who had never, in his whole life, learned to care for anyone else, not even his own daughter. But then the Jane he knew turned round, holding out a hot-water bottle for him to tighten the stopper, caught his eye, and uttered one of her still startling hoots of laughter.

'For heaven's sake,' she said, 'don't scowl like that! Just imagine if the wind changed—something terrible could happen to you. You might end up Lord Provost of Glasgow!'

And giving him a cheerful nudge in the ribs, she went off upstairs to look after her old friend.

When Jane came back, Philip and Susan had finished the washing-up, but then an argument arose between her and Susan over who would cook the lunch. Jane said, rather irritably, that she was perfectly well able to prepare a simple meal, but Susan got bossy, and threatened her with Dr Matheson. Eventually, to put an end to the bickering, Philip offered to cook frozen fish fingers and chips, and was despatched on his bicycle by a grateful Jane, to buy some. In his absence, Susan decided to launder her hockey clothes, but unfortunately the washing-machine had other ideas. When Philip came back, it had coughed up its contents all over the kitchen; Susan was trying to sweep the flood out of the back door with a broom, while Jane, perched high and dry on the table, gave her merry but quite useless advice.

Always, in later life, Philip would remember *The Mount* as a haunted house, forgetting that, on another level, a perfectly normal life had been lived in it, a life in which meals had been cooked, books read, telephone calls made and jokes exchanged, and where occasionally the washing-machine had gone on the blink, and been sick all over the kitchen. But now, certainly, the comical normality of this Saturday morning's events helped him, and Susan, to come to terms with last night's haunting ones—that, and the assurance that they were now approaching a journey's end. If there were other matters that had to be attended to this morning, they would go to Philip's house later in the day. They had the key, and they knew what they were going to find.

Philip cooked the chips and fish fingers, sniffed snootily when Jane said she hoped he wouldn't be offended if she had some Marmite instead, and put a large helping on a plate for Jo.

'But remember, Philip—no provocative remarks about God's Bountiful Deep Freeze,' warned Jane, spoiling his fun, as he had a good speech along these lines already prepared. He had to content himself with replying, 'Yes,

Miss Jane. Very good, Miss Jane,' in his best imitation of Jo's Highland voice, and having the satisfaction of hearing Jane remark to Susan, as he fled from the kitchen with the tray, 'I'm telling you—once I'm better able to run after him, that cheeky devil had better watch his step!'

Then, just after they had finished lunch, and Jane was looking forward to a quiet afternoon in her chair by the fire, Professor Watkins arrived to collect his manuscript, accompanied by two tiny and very unruly grandchildren. By her own frank admission, Jane was not good with babies, and, in answer to her amusing but frantic signals, there was nothing Philip and Susan could do, except offer to take the little creatures to the Park to play. With one thing and another, it was half-past three before they were at last free to set out for Tarbet Gardens.

But when they did get there, and had borrowed the key from Mrs Balloch, it was the work of seconds to open the little drawer, and remove the sealed envelope which, last night and long ago, Jane's proud, possessive father had secretively hidden away.

Silently, and wearily now, Susan and Philip walked back together through the Park. The chill, opaque dusk of December hung above the orange lights of the city, blackening the bare limbs of trees, and the vast silhouettes of the mansion houses on the hill. A full moon with frayed edges was trying to peer through, and, as the children crossed the railway bridge, they could see clearer lights above the embankment, in the windows of the Forbes' house, and other flats along the avenue. Only *The Mount*, with its ground floor windows obscured by winter foliage, reared up its head blindly into the night sky.

'No light in the drawing-room tonight,' remarked Susan, contentedly.

'Nor ever will be,' replied Philip. 'Not that light.'

When they got home, they passed the door of the dining-room, where Jane was dozing by the fire with an open book in her lap, and went quietly upstairs. And in Susan's room—because a check of the contents did seem wise, fifty years on—they slit open the outer envelope, tipping out

143

the folded letter, and the little white leather box. The ring was tiny, set with the smallest diamond imaginable; it was impossible that it could slip over the distended knuckles of an old woman's hand. But Jane would never want to wear it; having it would be enough. The letter they did not unfold. Already it had been read by one person who had no right to open it, and that was one too many.

'After supper, when she goes to bed, we'll take it down to her,' said Susan, slipping the ring lovingly back into its white velvet nest.

But, 'No,' said Philip harshly. 'Not me, thanks. It's bad enough she should have one of us watching her—not both of us, Sue. You can take it. It's women's stuff, engagement rings.'

He tried to sound tough and dismissive, but the truth was that this was something he couldn't bear to see.

Susan looked at him with troubled eyes.

'Philip,' she said, 'are we doing right in this? Remember what Jo said—that it would make Jane wretched again to know that her own father had wronged her so. I'd hate to hurt her.'

But Philip shook his head.

'It's all right,' he told her. 'She knows. Or, at least, she nearly knows. She told me one day that she suspected her father had once done her a most cruel wrong. Well—it couldn't be anything else, could it?'

'No,' said Susan. Slowly she put the letter, and the box with the ring, into her cardigan pocket. Then she made up her mind. 'All right,' she said. 'In the end, the only thing that matters is that she should know that Ewan loved her, and kept his word. She can't ever have been absolutely sure of that either, without the letter, and the ring. I'll take them to her gladly. Thanks, Philip.'

And so, later that night, when Jane was lying reading in her bed, Susan went down to her room. She was gone for some time, and Philip, who had intended to stay awake, could not. He fell asleep with the light on, and Susan, when she came upstairs at last, switched it off without disturbing him.

During the night, clouds from the Atlantic came softly up the Clyde. When Philip awoke on Sunday morning, the whole city of Glasgow was being swept by long grey curtains of rain. Out of a mouse-coloured sky it plashed down, hiding the cranes and the ships and the hills beyond, gushing in rivers down the gutters of Knightshill Road, slopping off the umbrellas of brave churchgoers, and people out fetching the Sunday papers. Around *The Mount*, the jungle was awash; branches dripped, quagmires formed, the old dry pool filled itself, and overflowed into the summer house. When Philip came down to breakfast, the weather seemed to have come indoors; the air in the hall was cold and moist, and there were damp patches all over the walls. Susan was alone in the dining-room, eating cereal under her great grandfather's baleful, but now powerless eye.

Philip sat down, poured himself a cup of coffee, and spread a slice of toast with butter and marmalade. Susan watched him thoughtfully.

'Well? How did she take it?' Philip asked at last, seeing that he would have to make the first move.

Susan did not immediately reply. She seemed to ponder the question as she poured herself more coffee, and stirred milk and sugar into it. Eventually she said, 'I hardly know. She didn't exactly jump for joy.'

'Did you expect her to?'

'I've no idea what I expected,' admitted Susan. 'It was a pretty unusual situation. She read the letter, and opened the box with the ring in it, but she didn't take it out, or touch it, even. She seemed completely stunned, as if she couldn't take it in at all.'

'That would be natural enough,' said Philip.

'Yes,' Susan agreed. 'But it was frightening, all the same. Poor love, she looked exactly the way she used to, before she got the message that laughing can be good for you. I was so scared that Jo was right, and that I'd done something unforgivable. But then—gosh, she didn't half get going. She took off her specs, and pushed the letter and the box away from her, and started asking me questions in the most nosy, un-Jane-like way. Talk about the Inquisition! I had only meant to tell her we had accidentally found a little key, and that you'd had the bright idea that it might open a drawer in an old desk at your house. But she wasn't having any of that. So when I realised she wasn't going to be put off, I started telling her what really happened, thinking she'd dismiss it as a lot of childish nonsense. You know how terribly rational she is, always saying there's a scientific explanation for everything. But the awful thing was—Philip, *she believed me*. She told me she didn't think she was the kind of person who would ever see a ghost, and that the house had never bothered her, but that long ago her mother had to send away a maid called Dora Gordon, who kept having hysterics because she saw strange children on the stair. And that her father had seen the ghosts of two children in that room upstairs, and had been frightened out of his wits. Well, I knew that, didn't I? And then she said that she had to get you and me out of this place as soon as possible, and that she would settle the matter with Mr Forbes today.'

'What has Mr Forbes got to do with it?' asked Philip, surprised.

'What indeed?' said Susan. 'Apparently he's the architect who's converted the other houses in the Avenue into flats, and he's just desperate to get his mitts on this one. He's offered Jane a lot of money, and if she wants, she can have one of those super new flats he's designed down at Ingram's Cross. Of course—being Jane—she's been thinking about it for weeks, and doing nothing.'

'Ingram's Cross?' squealed Philip delightedly. 'But that's near my place! It's just across the road!'

'Yes. Jane mentioned that. She said she'd been wondering whether she should move out of Glasgow, and get a cottage down the water, at Cardross, or Rhu—but now she doesn't want to, because of you, and your Maths lessons, and the weeks you're coming to stay. So it seems we're going to be neighbours, which certainly suits me.

Well, anyway—she calmed down after that, and thanked me in an odd, formal kind of way, for finding the ring and giving it to her. I told her that it was you who had found it, and that I'd never have had the guts to go into the room at night, if you hadn't made me. When I left her, she seemed quite cold and detached—but Jo is furious, and won't speak to me this morning, so I suspect that when she went in for their bedtime chat, she found Jane crying, and had to comfort her. These old souls really do love each other.'

Philip considered all of this for a while, then he said, 'But what about this morning, Sue? That's what really matters, isn't it? Have you seen Jane this morning?'

For the first time since he had come into the room, Susan smiled at him.

'Ah, this morning,' she said. 'You were asking me about last night. This morning's different. This morning she's sitting up in bed, actually eating toast and marmalade, and looking so happy, it does your heart good just to see her. And she says, when you've finished your breakfast, please will you go and talk to her?'

But Philip could not wait so long. He left his third slice of toast half eaten, his coffee half drunk, and went.

Outside, the world wept. There was a hole in the vestibule roof, and drips of water were falling rhythmically onto the tiled floor. The fog seemed to have moved through the hall, and begun to climb the stair. Philip crossed the dewy carpet to Jane's door, and knocked softly. Her voice called to him, and he went in.

'Good morning, Philip,' said Jane, joyfully. 'Isn't this a perfectly beautiful day?'